SHADOW OF INTRIGUE

Lantern Beach Romantic Suspense, Book 2

CHRISTY BARRITT

River Heights

Complete Book List

Squeaky Clean Mysteries:

#13 Cold Case: Clean Getaway

#14 Cold Case: Clean Sweep

While You Were Sweeping, A Riley Thomas Spinoff

The Sierra Files:

#1 Pounced

#2 Hunted

#3 Pranced

#4 Rattled

#5 Caged (coming soon)

The Gabby St. Claire Diaries (a Tween Mystery series):

The Curtain Call Caper

The Disappearing Dog Dilemma

The Bungled Bike Burglaries

The Worst Detective Ever

#1 Ready to Fumble

#2 Reign of Error

#3 Safety in Blunders

#4 Join the Flub

#5 Blooper Freak

#6 Flaw Abiding Citizen

#7 Gaffe Out Loud (coming soon)

Shadow of Intrigue
Storm of Doubt (coming soon)

Carolina Moon Series:
Home Before Dark
Gone By Dark
Wait Until Dark
Light the Dark
Taken By Dark

Suburban Sleuth Mysteries:
Death of the Couch Potato's Wife

Cape Thomas Series:
Dubiosity
Disillusioned
Distorted

Standalone Romantic Mystery:
The Good Girl

Suspense:
Imperfect
The Wrecking

Standalone Romantic-Suspense:

Keeping Guard

The Last Target

Race Against Time

Ricochet

Key Witness

Lifeline

High-Stakes Holiday Reunion

Desperate Measures

Hidden Agenda

Mountain Hideaway

Dark Harbor

Shadow of Suspicion

The Baby Assignment

Nonfiction:

Characters in the Kitchen

Changed: True Stories of Finding God through Christian Music (out of print)

The Novel in Me: The Beginner's Guide to Writing and Publishing a Novel (out of print)

Chapter One

LISA GARTH TRUDGED up the wooden outdoor steps, propping a paper bag full of groceries on her hip.

What a day.

What a week, for that matter.

If Lisa hadn't promised her friends Ty and Cassidy that she would help them out, she would be at home cuddled up with a book and a cup of tea right now. Instead, she'd fulfill her promise to fill in for them while they were away to celebrate Ty's mom's birthday.

Lisa reached the screened-in porch at the top of the stairs and froze. Slowly, she craned her neck to look behind her and scanned the darkness beyond the porch. Was someone watching her?

What? No. That was crazy. Who would be watching her out here?

John Linksi's image came to her mind, but she quickly pushed it out. The man might despise Lisa, but he had no reason to follow her and watch her.

She was just being paranoid.

As she stood exposed, a chilly wind swept around her, embracing her like a friend dead set on betrayal.

Lisa had forgotten just how cold it could feel on Lantern Beach—just as she did every year. Maybe the weather around here was like childbirth. If you remembered how painful it was, you'd never want to experience it again. At least, that was what she'd heard.

While some people looked forward to the quiet, isolated cold of the island's off-season, Lisa felt an unusual amount of dread this year. Her friends were all finding love and building new lives apart from her. Meanwhile, she sometimes felt as isolated as this island.

Shoving the thoughts aside, Lisa pounded at the door and waited.

She heard no signs of life inside the house and paused, contemplating her options.

A man named Braden Dillinger was coming to stay in Lantern Beach for the next week or two. He'd be using Ty and Cassidy's house while they were gone.

Ty had hired Lisa to act as hostess while Braden was here. It would provide her some extra cash in the slow season—and it would give her something to do. Since Lisa's restaurant, the Crazy Chefette, was only open on Saturdays and Sundays during the off-season, she had some time to spare.

Ty had also mentioned that his friend had some type of disability, but he hadn't clarified exactly what. It didn't matter. Braden's issues weren't any of Lisa's business.

She hadn't seen any vehicles outside the cottage, which seemed to confirm her initial theory that Braden hadn't arrived yet. That was another vague detail—his arrival time. Maybe Lisa should have asked more questions, but it was too late for that now.

Grabbing the spare key Ty had given her, she shoved it in the lock and opened the door.

Lisa stuck her head through the doorway and, just to be certain, called out, "Hello?"

No response.

Braden obviously wasn't here yet.

Perfect. This would give Lisa time to get dinner going so when Braden arrived, he could have a warm meal. She could greet him like the friendly hostess she was and then leave him in peace to eat.

Deed done.

Afterward, she'd drink her tea, read her book, and recover from her day.

Lisa set her bag on the kitchen counter and glanced around. Just like she'd figured, Ty and Cassidy had left everything tidy for their guest.

Her friends lived in this oceanside cottage, which was being transformed into what they called Hope House. Ty planned to make it a retreat center for military veterans who needed time away from their jobs—and their everyday lives—in order to heal both physically and emotionally.

The place wasn't quite ready to open yet for occupants. Ty had added a second story as well as reconfigured the layout downstairs. It was beautiful now with its whitewashed walls, beams on the ceiling, and sea-glass-colored accessories. The common area featured a combination kitchen, dining room, and living room.

Using her phone, Lisa turned on her favorite

playlist before pulling out the items she'd purchased at the store. She hadn't been sure what to make for Braden, but she'd decided on a chicken fajita pasta bake. Italian and Mexican food in one? It was the best of both worlds.

She sang along with "That's Amore" as she worked, trying to loosen up.

As soon as Lisa started to cook, she felt herself relax. Nothing calmed her like working in the kitchen—which was probably why she'd chosen to open a restaurant for a living. It was so much better than working in a lab.

Except for days like today. Days when John Linksi made her life miserable. She scowled as she remembered their earlier encounter.

She'd run into the man at the general store, where he'd berated her in front of other shoppers about what a horrible chef she was. She'd held her tears back while in the store, but as soon as she got into her car she'd let them flow.

Usually people's criticisms didn't get to her, but today it had felt different.

Probably because John used to be a food critic for *Good Eating* magazine. At one time, he'd been esteemed in the culinary community.

Now, he was just the town drunk. Tragedy had turned his life upside down five years ago, from what Lisa had heard. She didn't even know what had happened—only that John was never the same.

That still didn't give the man the right to speak to her the way he had today.

It was bad enough that he'd gone to every online site and written bad reviews. They were *scathing* reviews, for that matter. Then today he'd told everyone within earshot she was a hack, that her food tasted awful, and that she had no place here in Lantern Beach.

Usually, Lisa didn't believe him. But today the lies felt more like the truth, and she had no idea why. Maybe she was just in a funk. She'd call it the pre-winter doldrums. But she couldn't get his words out of her head.

While the food sizzled, Lisa walked to the window, shoved the curtain aside, and peered outside. Dunes stared back as well as part of the gravel lane leading toward the house. She didn't see anyone out here watching her, even though she thought she'd sensed someone else's presence when she'd arrived. Maybe it was just her mind playing tricks on her. Nor did she see any signs of head-lights on the road in the distance.

Just when would Braden get here? Lisa supposed if he arrived too late, she would just leave the food out, and Braden could warm it at his convenience. She wouldn't get any bonus points as hostess of the year, but she had to be flexible here. After all, tea and a good book were calling.

As she turned back to the kitchen, a creak sounded behind her.

Before she could react, an arm looped around her throat. It tightened and squeezed like an anaconda capturing its prey.

Lisa's heart rate ricocheted as she tried to get a breath, to comprehend what was happening.

"Who are you?" a gruff voice barked into her ear. "And how did you find me?"

Braden Dillinger's adrenaline pumped so hard that he could feel the veins in his neck throbbing as he put the intruder into a chokehold.

Intruder?

No, that word made her seem too unassuming. This woman was a killer. An assassin. A terrorist. Braden wasn't sure which yet.

"Please, let go of me." The woman's voice

sounded strained against his arm. "You're hurting me."

She clawed at him, her nails digging into his skin. Braden didn't care. He'd been through far worse on the battlefield and in warzones—places so horrible that they didn't exist on paper. He had more enemies than he could count, and most were nameless and faceless. That made everything even more difficult.

"I'm just here to cook," the woman rasped, struggling beneath his hold on her.

She tried to fight, yet her strength seemed subdued—more so than Braden had expected for a professional.

Something tried to register in his brain, but the thought wouldn't fully form.

Had she said she was here to cook? A likely excuse.

"Who are you?" Braden demanded, still not letting his guard down.

He couldn't.

Not when someone was trying to kill him. There had already been a hit-and-run attempt, along with his bank account being drained. Whoever was behind the attempts on his life wouldn't stop until they got what they wanted:

Braden dead.

And Braden wouldn't put it past them to send a beautiful woman to do the job. No, he knew who was behind the threats: a network of criminals who thought Braden had wronged them.

And that made it harder.

Because it meant there wasn't just one face he had to watch for. No, the person sent to kill him could be anyone.

The gratingly happy background music was a nice touch. The tune made the woman seem innocent, as did her jeans and black T-shirt. When he'd stepped from the shower and heard movement in the house, Braden had known his enemy had found him and was making his next play.

"I'm . . . Lisa Garth." Her voice cracked with desperation. "Ty Chambers . . . hired me."

Braden's grip loosened. Ty? Had his friend told him he was hiring someone to come here?

Braden squeezed his eyes shut and whipped his head back and forth in short, jerky motions. If only the action would shake his brain back into proper function.

Was this a trick? A distraction? Or had Braden's mind failed him again?

"Please." The woman's hands continued to claw

his arm, and her voice sounded thin enough to break. "You're hurting me. And dinner is going to burn. Let me go."

She sounded earnest and scared. Now that she'd mentioned it, Braden did smell onions and peppers. Could she be telling the truth?

Cautiously, he released the woman and stepped back.

That was when Braden caught a glimpse of her face.

Her lovely face and bright eyes that matched her sweet-smelling blonde hair. He had noticed the scent just seconds earlier. Watermelon.

One of his favorite aromas.

But there was also another scent. Was that patchouli?

An odd combination.

The woman's eyes widened as her survival instincts seemed to kick in. As she turned to him, she grabbed a huge whelk shell from the end table beside her and held it toward him like brass knuckles. The fear was still in her eyes, but a new emotion was there also. Self-preservation, maybe?

But did she really think she could defend herself with a whelk shell?

"Who are you?" The veins at her neck bulged,

and her chest rose and fell with rapid breaths as she stared him down. "Maybe you're the one who should be explaining."

"I'm Braden." He took a step back, a wave of regret washing over him.

What had he been thinking? How had this situation escalated so quickly? But after he'd stepped out of the bathroom and seen this woman, he'd been sure she was the one behind those threats. One of the last messages he'd received had said Braden would be taken unaware. The next thing he knew, he'd found this stranger in the house and . . .

"My friend Ty owns this place," he finally said.

The woman glanced at his arms, and confusion crossed her gaze. "But . . ."

"But what?" Braden wasn't sure what she was getting at or why she looked so puzzled.

She shook her head a little too adamantly. "Nothing. Ty should have told you about me. I'm Lisa, and I'm supposed to be acting as hostess while you're here. I own a restaurant on the island. The Crazy Chefette."

Braden squinted, trying to remember the last conversation with his friend. Had Ty said that? Probably. His memory felt so fuzzy right now. Braden *had* told Ty about the issues he'd been having since returning from the Middle East. Memory lapses were just one of many. Yet sometimes Braden would have rather lost a limb than live with this kind of uncertainty.

"You can put the shell down." Braden raised his hands, a mixture of apology and mild amusement in his voice. "I'm sorry. I . . . I don't know what to say."

Lisa narrowed her eyes, still holding her weapon. Anger flared in her gaze again. "I'm sorry is not going to do it. I thought you were going to kill me."

"I thought you'd broken in. I was in the shower, so I didn't hear you come inside. I came down and . . ."

"You thought I'd broken in and started to cook for you?" Disbelief stretched through her voice.

Braden squeezed his eyes shut. It didn't make much sense now that she said it that way. But his brain . . . it was a minefield within itself lately. Things that had once seemed normal and logical were now out of whack.

Lisa stared at him, obviously still processing their conversation. Finally, she lowered the shell onto the table, and her shoulders seemed to relax— but only by a fraction.

"There was no car out front." Her voice cracked as she raised her chin.

"I hired someone to drop me off. I . . . I don't drive right now." He couldn't. Not with the medication he was taking as he tried to manage his symptoms.

She stared at him still, as if trying to decide her next course of action. Finally, she released a long breath and crossed her slender arms. "Listen, I don't know what's going on. But I don't want any part of it. I'm going to finish cooking this meal, and then I'm gone. I'm out of your hair. I'll just have to tell Ty that it didn't work out for me to play hostess."

Regret panged inside Braden again. He really knew how to mess things up, didn't he? He could have easily hurt this woman. No, done more than hurt her. Thank God, he hadn't. "I understand."

She hurried back to the kitchen and scraped some veggies and chicken strips into a bowl filled with pasta. She furiously began stirring the food before shoveling it all into a casserole dish.

Braden took a step back and raked a hand through his hair. He'd never intended on scaring an innocent woman. If only his brain worked the way it used to. If only war hadn't messed him up and changed him into a different person from the one he'd once been. On his off time, he used to enjoy football, and fishing, and tailgate parties. Now, his life centered around simply functioning.

He'd hoped coming here to Lantern Beach might help him to see things more clearly.

And buy him some more time before danger came knocking again.

His shoulders slumped.

How was he going to explain this to Ty? He'd trusted Braden with his home and . . . well, Braden had nearly gone off the deep end and hurt one of Ty's friends.

He glanced across the room to the kitchen. Lisa continued working, adding some freshly grated cheese to the top of a casserole dish. It was a wonder she hadn't fled—but based on her tight, jerky actions, she still might.

The petite woman had some fire in her—and some stick-to-itiveness. Her hair swished around her shoulders as she worked, her trim figure moving with confidence, like she knew exactly what she was doing.

"So, you were a Navy SEAL?" Lisa's voice didn't sound especially friendly, more like she was going through the motions of being polite as she hurried through her tasks so she could leave as quickly as possible. Or maybe she was trying to gauge just how dangerous he was.

Which was understandable after what Braden had just done.

"No, not a SEAL," he said, his voice dull. He leaned against the counter, a comfortable distance away. "I was Special Forces."

She stole a skeptical glance over her shoulder. "There's a difference?"

Braden shrugged, heaviness still surrounding him as he thought about his past and the problems that had led him to where he was today. "Yeah, actually, there is."

He'd done special assignments. Some of them off the books. And usually he worked solo.

His whole military career had been compli-cated, so it only made sense that his war injuries were equally as complex. He'd perplexed all the professionals who'd tried to treat him.

Lisa looked over her shoulder as she placed some of her dishes into the soapy water filling the sink. "That just needs to bake for about twenty minutes so all the cheese melts together. Then you can eat, and I'll be out of your hair."

Before Braden could say anything else, his phone buzzed.

He glanced at the screen.

People can run but they can't hide. Wise people watch their backs. Revenge is within reach.

Chapter Two

LISA LEANED against the kitchen counter, trying to catch her breath. Blood still pulsed through her, rushing with adrenaline-fueled intensity. Yes, her day had gotten worse.

First, she'd been bemoaning her love life. Then John had insulted her talent. Now this man had threatened her physical well-being.

That pretty much covered everything and hit on every important facet of her life, other than her faith.

She glanced over her shoulder. Braden had disappeared several minutes ago after his phone had buzzed. Not only that, but his face had gone pale. Had something else triggered him? Would

Bruce Banner become the Incredible Hulk and nearly kill her again?

She shuddered.

Just what was this guy's story?

It didn't matter. She was just glad Braden had disappeared for a moment. Lisa could use the space. They'd attempted small talk, but it had been awkward at best. What she really wanted was to get out of here.

She should have left after he released her from the chokehold. So why hadn't she? Because she liked to finish what she started and didn't want to waste food? She knew that wasn't it.

More likely it was because, beneath Braden's abrupt reaction to seeing her, something about the man looked so lost and bewildered and genuinely confused. Lisa's mom had always told her that having such a soft heart for people would be the death of her. Maybe her mom was right.

Ten minutes later, Braden emerged from the back. His timing was perfect—the casserole had just come out. Lisa could serve it, and her job was done. She'd be out of here soon.

Braden quietly sat at the table with no explanation about his disappearance.

Lisa plated a piece of the pasta dish and pushed it across the kitchen table to Braden. "Here you go. Now that the food is ready, I'm going to run. I hope you get some rest and find what you're looking for here."

She heard how fast her words came out and cringed. She wouldn't earn any acting awards, but she didn't care. Her life had flashed before her eyes earlier. She didn't want any repeats.

As she turned to walk away, Braden touched her wrist—only lightly, thank goodness. Because Lisa was ready to flee. To run fast and hard. To chew out her friends for ever asking her to do this. The man's touch only drove home that point even more.

As his hand remained at her wrist, her breath caught with trepidation. Lisa's gaze flickered to Braden. To his square face. His light brown hair that was damp and tousled. To the barely there beard that actually just might be the result of not shaving for a day instead of following a trend. His eyes were brown, his brow seemed permanently set in contemplation, and his skin seemed like it should be darker, tanner than it was.

What kind of secrets was this man hiding?

"Listen, I really am sorry." Braden's voice

sounded hoarse with regret as he dragged his gaze up to hers.

Lisa opened her mouth to respond, but her mind went blank. What should she say? She wasn't ready yet to tell him everything was okay and he was forgiven. Instead, she pulled away from his touch and stepped toward the door.

"Have a good evening, Braden."

Once Lisa was out of Ty's house and standing on the screened-in porch, she released the breath she held. She paused long enough to let the cold air slap some sense into her.

It seemed so unlike Ty and Cassidy to put her in a situation like that. Her friends were good people —the kind who looked out for her best interests. What had gone wrong?

She wasn't going to stick around any longer to ponder it. No, she wanted to get far away from Braden Dillinger—for good. She had enough to worry about without adding him to her list.

Lisa hurried back to her car, climbed inside, and hit the locks.

But before she pulled out, she grabbed her phone and dialed Ty's number. She hated to interrupt him on his trip, but . . . she couldn't let this slide.

"Hey, Lisa," Ty answered. "What's going on?"

The former Navy SEAL was tougher than nails yet the all-American boy next door, rolled into one. Lisa was so glad he'd found Cassidy. The two were obviously meant for each other.

She licked her lips, still in shock. "Hey, sorry for the intrusion. But I just met your friend."

"Braden? He's a great guy, isn't he?" Ty's voice sounded sincere. Which only added to her confusion.

Great guy wasn't exactly how Lisa would describe Braden. "I thought he was going to kill me. Like, literally kill me, not the cute little expression people use when someone's really mad at them."

She felt the need to throw that last part in, just to clarify.

"What?" Ty's voice rose with surprise.

"He put me in a chokehold." Lisa cringed as she remembered the feeling of Braden's thick arm around her neck. The man was large—in height and stature. He was practically made of strapping muscles that were designed for destruction or protection. She wasn't sure which.

Her bets were on destruction right now.

If he hadn't snapped back to his senses when he did, the man *could* have killed her. The thought kept slamming back into Lisa's mind, as if she could forget.

"That doesn't sound like the Braden I know." Ty lowered his voice with regret. "I knew he had issues, but not those kinds of issues. If I had any idea . . . I'm so sorry, Lisa. Are you okay?"

"I'm fine. He said he thought I was an intruder. I didn't even know he was there. There was no car out front or anything." The whole story sounded strange and far-fetched. But it really had happened. Lisa guessed that would teach her to go into someone else's house with too many assumptions.

"He's a good guy," Ty said. "But I know he wanted to come here to get away from things. Maybe something changed since I saw him last. Maybe the things he wanted to get away from were more serious than he let on."

"Maybe," Lisa muttered, trying to shut out her compassion.

"Either way, don't worry about acting as hostess. Braden can fend for himself, okay?"

"Got it." That worked for her because she had no desire to interact with the man again. "Anyway —have fun. Tell Cassidy hello."

"I will. Thanks again, Lisa."

After she ended the call, Lisa leaned back into her seat.

She needed to get home and far away from this Braden guy. She wasn't thinking clearly.

As she put her car in reverse, she paused.

Was that a shadow moving on the dune outside Ty's place?

Lisa couldn't be sure. It was so dark out there.

No . . . she squinted. There it was again.

It was definitely a shadow.

Braden, she realized. Braden must have gone outside. Was he watching her now? Planning another surprise attack?

Her heart throbbed in her ears, and all her muscles tightened at the thought.

Lisa had to get out of here before he saw her again and got any ideas.

She zoomed from the driveway.

Good riddance.

If she never saw that man again, it would be too soon.

"Yeah, I'm sorry." Braden moved away from the

window, where he'd watched the car pull down the street. Lisa. That poor woman. He'd scared the daylights out of her. Regret bit deep. "I don't know what happened."

"What's going on?" Ty asked on the other end of the phone line. "It doesn't even sound like you to do something like that."

Braden raked a hand through his hair as he remembered the encounter. "I have no idea. I just . . . I thought someone had broken into the house, and I reacted. I reacted *poorly*. I feel terrible about it."

"Are you still having memory problems, Braden?" Ty's voice dipped lower.

"Yeah, I am. I'm hoping some time away from the stress at home will help. That's what my therapist said, at least."

"Is there anything you're not telling me?"

Braden ground his teeth together in thought. It wasn't fair that he'd kept his friend in the dark about the threats against him. But he'd really thought that by coming here, he'd be getting away from those concerns.

"Members of The Revolt have been threatening me."

"The Revolt? That's the terrorist group you helped to take down."

"I know. And word has it that my name leaked to them. The few remaining members are trying to find me and exact revenge."

"What? How would they have gotten your name?"

"Maybe we have a leak. Who knows."

"Why do you think they're after you?"

"Someone's been sending me threatening text messages."

"Did you tell the police?"

"They can't trace the number."

"Is that it?"

Braden squeezed his eyes shut. "Someone tried to run me off the road also, and my bank account was drained."

"Braden . . . why didn't you tell me?"

He rubbed his temple, feeling the beginning of a headache. "Because I feel like I'm losing my mind. Just when I start thinking clearly . . . something else happens and everything feels fuzzy. I'm a soldier, Ty. I'm supposed to be able to take care of myself. But I can't even prove these guys are behind this or that these threats are even real and not my imagination."

"Are you still seeing your therapist?"

"I am. I'm trying to back off. I want to move on, Ty."

"I can understand that. Just don't move on too early."

"Yeah, I know." *You can't rush healing.* That's what Braden's therapist always reminded him. "Either way, I don't think anyone followed me here. I tried to cover all my tracks. I really just wanted to get away from trouble . . . I hope I didn't bring it with me."

"I hope you didn't either. In the meantime, I don't want Lisa going back to the house. Not if that might happen again."

"I totally understand. And I'm real sorry about your friend. She seemed nice." It didn't matter how many times Braden said it, it would never be enough.

"Lisa's one of the nicest people you'll meet. Anyway, call me if you need me, Braden. Or you can call my friends Austin or Wes. They said they would be there. I left their numbers on the fridge."

"Got it. I appreciate everything."

Braden ended the call and walked toward the window again. The dish Lisa had so carefully prepared sat cold on the table. He didn't have the appetite to eat right now.

His chest roiled with unrest. This wasn't what he wanted for his trip here. No, Braden had visions of embracing peace and relaxation. Of coming to terms with his life. He still had hope that things would change.

But that was looking less and less likely.

He continued to peer outside, trying to put that text out of his mind.

People can run but they can't hide. Wise people watch their backs. Revenge is within reach.

He really had gotten that text, hadn't he? Or had he imagined that also?

The weight of his memory problems hung heavy on his shoulders and on his mind. Most days, he tried his best to push through. But, at times, he let his mind wander to the future. When he thought about spending the rest of his life like this, despair began to consume him. He couldn't handle the thought that there might not be an end in sight. And he felt like hope was slipping further and further away with every moment his problems continued.

Movement outside caught his eye.

Was someone out there on the dunes in the distance?

Was it Lisa? Had she come back for some reason? No, he would have heard her car. Seen the headlights.

His muscles tightened even more.

The text echoed in his mind again. *Revenge is within reach.*

Had the person trying to kill him found him here? Was this the place whoever was threatening him would end it all?

Maybe that was the perfect plan on his enemy's part. Here, no one would miss Braden for days. Maybe not even after that—not until Ty arrived back home.

The shadow moved again, the motion so subtle that Braden wondered if the wind had simply shifted something on the dune. But he knew that wasn't the case.

Braden pulled his gun from his waistband—he'd grabbed it from his suitcase after he'd gotten the text—and he stepped onto the screened-in porch. "Who's out there?"

No one responded.

"Who is it?" he asked again. "I know you're there."

The shadow moved one more time.

Before he could find the source of his unease again, something loud popped beside him. Again. And again. And again.

And suddenly, Braden felt like he was back on the battlefield.

Chapter Three
_____

LISA SAT on her couch with a cup of tea beside her, a blanket over her, and a book in hand.

Her concentration was shot. All she could think about was the feel of Braden's arm around her neck. The fleeting fear that her life could end. The memory of the sheer power in the man's muscles.

She tried to stop replaying it. She really did. But her thoughts wouldn't cooperate.

Just as she lowered her book, ready to admit defeat, her phone buzzed. She looked down at the screen and read a text message from her friend Skye.

Did you meet your prince charming tonight?

Lisa let out a quick laugh and rolled her eyes before typing back: **Not quite.**

Ever since Skye had found true love, she was determined that Lisa would be next. She'd been wrong on this one. Really wrong.

I heard about John, Skye texted.

Lisa frowned.

Great. Word had gotten around town about their exchange in the general store earlier.

Ever since the Crazy Chefette had been named one of the Ten Most Fun Restaurants on the North Carolina Coast, John had been determined to let her know any praise the critics had given her had been wrong.

Lisa texted: **Yeah, it wasn't fun.**

Skye texted again: **John's a jerk. We'll have to chat about it more tomorrow. But don't worry about him in the meantime. He just wants attention.**

Will do, Lisa typed back. **Talk more tomorrow.**

Lisa put her phone down, pulled up the blanket around her, and took another sip of her tea.

She glanced around her cozy apartment. It was located in the space above the Crazy Chefette, and she loved it here. Dark brown beams crossed overhead, complimenting the intricate woodwork around the windows and the rich wood paneling on the ceiling.

The place was by no means modern or updated. But Lisa still liked it. The building had been a Coast Guard station at one time. Now the bottom floor was her restaurant and the second story her home.

"Here you are," she muttered to herself. "Alone. You should just accept this as your fate."

It wasn't that Lisa really believed in fate. It was just that she knew the statistics. She'd read the Bridget Jones series, where the facts were discussed *ad nauseam*.

The older she got, the less chance she would ever get married.

And she would turn thirty next week.

Maybe it wouldn't be so bad if winter hadn't come. Suddenly, Lisa was questioning all of her independence, her choices, and even her ability to reason.

She loved it here. Loved her restaurant. Loved her friends.

But there was just something missing.

Get over it, Lisa. Maybe this is your lot in life. And

that's okay. We all have different paths, and maybe yours is sheer and utter isolation for now. Consider it a type of hibernation. But then you can emerge in the spring, open the Crazy Chefette full-time again after a long winter hiatus, and bloom.

Out of her group of friends here on Lantern Beach, Lisa was the one who'd always wanted to get married and have kids and live the quintessential American dream. Yet she was the one furthest from the goal.

Becoming a family woman didn't appear to be on the horizon. Nope, there weren't even any possibilities in sight.

Lisa had figured she would meet someone at college. When she didn't, she figured she'd meet someone on the job. When she didn't, well . . . she moved here and figured Lantern Beach would be the best place to meet someone.

But she hadn't.

She supposed she was married to her restaurant. It was just that during these winter months when work wasn't busy . . . she felt restless. Maybe even a little lonely.

What was wrong with her tonight? Lisa let out a laugh and shook her head.

She turned back to her book and tried to read,

but the words weren't even registering in her mind. Her concentration was definitely shot.

She sat up straight, her senses suddenly on alert as a sound cut through the silence.

What was that?

She heard it again.

Something breaking.

Glass?

Had someone shattered one of her windows downstairs?

Her pulse raced.

What if someone had broken in? Were they trying to steal something from the restaurant— money from the register, most likely? Or was it for another purpose?

She remembered the feeling of being watched earlier.

Lisa's heart raced even faster.

She couldn't just sit here like a deer during open season.

She grabbed her phone and dialed Mac MacArthur. He was filling in for Cassidy, the police chief, until she returned from Texas. The man had headed the police force here for decades until he retired. But even in his retirement, he'd kept an eye on the town. It was only natural that Mac step in for Cassidy while she was gone.

Mac promised to come right out. Until then, Lisa pulled the blanket higher and waited for the sound of footsteps pounding up the stairs toward her. Waited for another encounter that would have her life flashing before her eyes.

Please, Lord, protect me. And don't let this day get any worse. I didn't think it could, but I feel like I'm on a collision course of being proven wrong.

"I didn't see anyone outside." Mac stood just inside by Lisa's back door in the area where deliveries were made to the left and the stairs to her living quarters rose to the right.

At the moment, broken shards of glass from the bottom pane of the window atop her door littered the floor. Mac had shown up ten minutes after Lisa called, looking like he'd already been dressed and ready to work.

The man was thin and wiry, with white hair and an even whiter goatee. His eyes always sparkled, and he lived to bring justice where justice was due.

Lisa crossed her arms, still feeling uneasy. Her

mind had gone to the worst places—places where someone had broken in with plans to attack her. Could Braden have done this? John?

She cleared her throat, realizing her thoughts might make her seem paranoid. Maybe this was all just an accident. "Good to know that whoever did this is gone."

Mac slipped on a glove, stooped down, and used tweezers to pull something from the wall in front of the door. Lisa gasped when she recognized the object clutched in the shiny metallic tool. But the words wouldn't leave her mouth to confirm what her eyes had seen.

"It's a bullet." Mac straightened and examined her again as he slipped the bullet into an evidence bag and sealed it. "You didn't hear gunfire?"

Lisa shook her head, wondering how she'd missed that. "Only the glass breaking."

"Someone could have used a silencer, I guess."

She tugged her sweater more closely around her as a chilly breeze slithered through the window. "Why would anyone do this?"

Mac sighed and rested his hands at his belt. "You know how people are. Some people just get bored this time of year. There's nothing else for them to do so they cause trouble."

"Well, that trouble is going to cost me money." This was the time of year when cash got tight. Unforeseen repairs weren't what she wanted.

Mac frowned. "Unfortunately, that happens. But I'm glad you weren't hurt."

"Me too." Lisa shivered and wrapped her arms more tightly around herself. This day couldn't be over quickly enough.

"You have some wood left over from hurricane season?" Mac asked. "The pieces you put over your windows?"

"I do. They're in the shed behind the building."

"I'll help you cover the door so you can rest a little easier tonight," he said. "But first I'd like to check out the rest of your place."

"To make sure no one is inside?" Her voice sounded thin, even to her own ears. The thought of someone lurking in the dark recesses of her home was horrifying.

"And to make sure nothing has been stolen."

"Of course."

Lisa followed behind Mac as they inspected her space. She was glad Mac was here—she didn't want to face this place alone, not until she knew it was safe.

Thankfully, everything was clear and nothing appeared to have been taken.

She and Mac paused in the kitchen after their walk-through.

"Can I get you a piece of cake?" Lisa asked. "I have some of your favorite—cayenne and chocolate."

He grinned. "You know I can't resist some of that."

She cut him a piece, plated it, and gingerly placed it on the table in front of him. Mac wasted no time grabbing his fork and taking a bite. Delight stretched across his face.

"Delicious, as always. You, my dear, are a culinary genius."

Satisfaction warmed her. "I'm glad you like it."

Mac studied her face as he took another bite. "You can't think of anyone who would want to shoot at your restaurant, can you? I mean, I'm assuming this is random. Is there anything I should know?"

Braden's image flashed through her mind. No. Braden had no reason to break her window.

Sure, he'd put her in a chokehold earlier, but that didn't mean the man had tracked her here and tried to scare her. What sense would that make?

It would make *no* sense. However, Lisa did give him the name of her restaurant. What had she been thinking?

Then John's image flashed in her mind. Could he want to ruin her that much? He seemed to have a personal vendetta but . . .

"Lisa?" Mac asked, pulling her back to the present.

Whom should she mention? Anyone?

"I did have a confrontation in the grocery store today," Lisa said, pulling her sweater over her hands.

"I heard. John?"

She nodded, hating how quickly word had spread.

"I'll talk to him." Mac finished and pushed his plate aside. "Unfortunately, being a jerk isn't a crime. It should be, don't you think?"

"Absolutely."

"I'll check his alibi for tonight, just to be sure."

Lisa crossed her arms. "Thank you."

"If you need anything, you call me, okay? I'll be right here."

"I always appreciate you, Mac. Thanks so much."

As soon as he left, loneliness consumed her

again. Why did everything seem to be screaming that she was in danger and that her life was falling apart?

Because, if she was honest with herself, sometimes she believed the lies. Believed that she was a hack. That her restaurant was terrible. That she had no place on this island.

Chapter Four

BRADEN OPENED his eyes and blinked.

Where was he?

Memories of Iraq filled his mind, and he waited to hear the sounds of the warzone. Hurried footsteps as soldiers ran for cover. Distant bombs. Urgent shouting.

Instead, he heard . . . birds squawking overhead. Frogs chirping. Waves crashing.

Waves? Where could he be? His skin felt entirely too chilly for the Middle East. The sounds were all wrong. Yet his body felt like it had been through a battle.

He raised his head, and his fingers rubbed against the rough wood beneath him.

Wood? He'd expected dry, gritty dirt. Rough cement. Maybe even sand.

As Braden pushed himself up, he soaked in the decking around him. The screened-in windows. The swing swaying in the breeze.

The darkness had fled. Despite the cold, the sun glared bright and strong, coming right at him from the east.

Lantern Beach, he remembered.

Last night flashed back to him. The woman who'd come into the house. The way he'd attacked her. The fear on her face.

He recalled stepping onto the screened-in porch, seeing a shadow, and then hearing . . . gunfire.

He flinched just thinking about it.

Had someone fired at him?

And he'd gotten that ominous text, the one that had indicated someone knew Braden was here on Lantern Beach. Someone unknown. Faceless. Dangerous.

He sucked in a breath and lumbered to his feet like a drunk who'd passed out cold. Once standing and steady, Braden glanced around, searching for evidence he wasn't crazy.

He checked the screens for bullet holes, but they appeared intact.

He checked the siding. There was nothing.

Braden had definitely heard *something*.

He squeezed the skin between his eyes. He must have blacked out because he couldn't remember anything after he'd heard those bangs. And, last he recalled, it had been dark outside. Now it was morning. Braden had lost a good eight or nine hours.

Eight or nine *hours*.

He ran a hand over his face, hating this person he'd become. Hating that he was no longer the strong, capable man who let nothing ever stand in his way.

Now he was at the mercy of his mind. At the mercy of circumstances and prescription drugs and whatever the breeze blew in.

He'd been trusting that God would bring him through this, but some days felt more uncertain.

Like now.

Lord, please help me. I don't know what else to do. I'm at the end of the rope, and my hands are slipping. If I let go . . . I don't know if I'll ever be able to grab hold of any kind of lifeline again.

Braden took a few steps and nearly collapsed on

the swing. His body felt heavy with burdens that no one could see but that Braden could feel—as if an albatross hung around his neck.

Pulling out his phone, he held it. His hands trembled again, reminding him of his brokenness once more.

Like he needed more reminders.

He hit the number of his psychologist, and a moment later Dr. Rick Larson's voice came on the line.

"Braden," he started, his voice warm and friendly. "You got to your retreat center okay, I guess."

Dr. Larson had been working with Braden for more than a year. Braden had been friends with Thomas, Dr. Larson's son. Four years ago, Thomas had been killed when a training exercise went wrong. Braden had remained close to the family, and it only made sense that Dr. Larson would treat him.

"I got here okay. But I already had an episode." Braden's stomach clenched at the memories.

Dr. Larson was quiet a moment. "Did you take your meds?"

"Yeah, I took them before I hopped in the shower yesterday."

"Make sure you take them. Missing even one dosage can set you back."

"I know." Braden had heard it enough times before. Yet he still missed a dose on occasion or thought he could cope without the pills. But the doctor insisted they would eventually help him regain his life.

"This time away from everything will be good for you, Braden. The change of environment, getting away from the reminders of war . . . I think this will be the start of a season of renewal in your life."

"I hope so." Braden gripped the phone and stared out at the beach. Despite the relaxing sounds of the ocean in the background, his lungs were still tight—almost as tight as his muscles.

"What caused the episode? I'm assuming you blacked out again. Any idea what triggered it?"

Memories pummeled him. "I thought someone was shooting at me."

Dr. Larson was quiet again. "I see. Why did you think that, Braden? Did something happen?"

Braden squeezed his eyes shut. "I heard . . . I heard something."

"It could be your mind playing tricks on you."

"I know." Braden thought about that fact nearly

every waking minute. No one needed to remind him.

"Try to take it easy. And, again, don't forget your meds. Call me if you need anything else, okay? I'm just a few hours away."

"Got it, doc. Thanks." Braden hoped it wouldn't come to that.

He paused for a second and contemplated telling Dr. Larson about attacking Lisa. He decided not to. Not now. No, he needed to sort some things out for himself first.

He ended the call and stood. Maybe a walk would help.

He lumbered down the stairs, knowing he needed a jacket in this temperature, but he didn't care right now. Maybe the blast of cool ocean air would be good for him, like a slap in the face that would bring him back to his senses.

As Braden reached the bottom step, he crossed the driveway at the base of the stairway and started toward a path over the dune.

Before he got there, he paused and squatted. He picked up some papers on the ground.

Firecrackers.

Someone had set off firecrackers beneath the house last night, he realized.

Why would someone do that? As a prank? Did they think no one was here?

Or *was* there more to this story?

Braden didn't know. And he didn't like it.

But he was going to keep his eyes open.

Because trouble could have followed him here. Could be watching him right now. Could be waiting for the perfect time to strike.

And Braden wasn't here to hide. No, he would fight. Maybe—just maybe—his nightmare would end, once and for all.

But first he had to figure out who was behind this.

Lisa finished prepping all her food for the day and glanced at her watch. She would open for business in ten minutes, and Tammy, her waitress, still wasn't here, nor was she answering her phone.

Great.

Lisa hadn't been that busy these past few weeks. But still, good help was hard to find. Knowing Lisa's luck, the place would be slammed today. She'd already lost the majority of her employees when everyone except for island full-timers had left for the winter. In the summer, an influx of teens came here, looking for a fun summer job at the beach and a change of scenery. But that season had passed.

Despite that, Lisa was glad it was Saturday and her restaurant was open today. She needed something to occupy her thoughts. She couldn't stop replaying her encounter with Braden last evening, not to mention the broken window and John. In fact, she'd hardly slept all night.

Instead, she'd listened for creaks and shattering glass. She'd searched for hidden figures and watching eyes and men waiting to put her in chokeholds.

Still gripping her phone, she glanced at her watch. It was time for this show to get started, with or without Tammy. Right when Lisa unlocked the door and turned over the sign out front to read "Open," someone stepped inside.

She sucked in a deep breath and drew herself back, her defenses instantly going up.

Braden.

He nodded, almost awkwardly as he stood at the entrance wearing jeans, an olive-colored shirt, and a thick khaki jacket. "I've been outside for an hour, waiting until you opened."

Lisa's throat suddenly felt dry and achy. Maybe she should call Mac. Or even Wes or Austin. They'd be here in a flash to help her out.

Instead, she swallowed hard. The fact remained that this man could break her neck in five seconds flat if he set his mind to it. She doubted anyone could stop him if he set his mind to something.

She wouldn't jump the gun. Not yet.

She rubbed her neck, trying to ease the ache there. "You should have called. I would have told you my hours, and you might not be so cold right now. I feel terrible that you've been out here for so long."

Her voice sounded stiff and breathless, but no amount of optimism could change that.

Braden shifted again and dipped his head, not seeming as much like a mercenary today. "I . . . uh, I really just wanted to apologize again for yesterday."

The man sounded sincere. He looked sincere. Maybe he *was* sincere.

But Lisa reminded herself not to be too trusting. Being too trusting got her in trouble.

"It's done and over with, so don't worry about it," she finally said, determined not to draw this conversation out any more than it needed to be.

"I wanted to give you this." Braden held out an outstretched hand with something shiny in his palm.

Lisa picked up what appeared to be a bullet casing and squinted with alarm. "I don't understand."

Was this some kind of threat? His way of admitting he was the one who'd shot out her window last night?

"I carry one of these with me wherever I go," Braden said, jamming his hands into his pockets. "It reminds me of the battlefield. Of how hard that time in my life was, but how necessary for the bigger picture—the picture outside myself. When I think about that, it gives me the strength to make the right choices, even when those choices are unpleasant or hard."

Lisa's heart panged as emotion began clogging up inside her. Her fear was unfounded. The man had come with good intentions. "That's really beautiful."

Braden's expression looked so earnest and solemn that he almost seemed like a soldier coming to announce a death on the battlefield. Why was the man so perplexing to her? She didn't want to like him—yet she felt herself rooting for him at the same time.

"I was hoping you'd accept it as a sign of apology. It's my way of saying that I messed up but that I want to do the right thing."

"Of course I accept your apology." Lisa took the casing, stared at it one more time, and put it into the pocket of her jeans. The gesture really was sweet.

"Thank you."

She peered beyond Braden into the parking lot as a question hit her. "How did you get here? You don't have a car."

He shrugged. "I walked."

Her eyes widened as she pictured the distance between Ty's place and here. It was probably two miles. "Long walk."

"I don't have anything else to do."

She took a better look at Braden. He had circles under his eyes. His hair was tousled. His eyes were bloodshot.

Yesterday, he had looked off his game—or was it off his rocker? But today he looked even worse, only in a somber, heavy-hearted way. She just couldn't figure this guy out. Unfortunately, part of her wanted to.

Maybe he was like some scientific experiment that she wanted to get to the bottom of. Unanswered questions had always fascinated her. It was one of the reasons she originally wanted to become a scientist.

"No offense, but you look pretty horrible."

"I feel pretty horrible." Braden looked as if he tried to smile but couldn't.

Guilt bit into Lisa. She should let the man leave. Forget the forlorn look in his eyes. Put space between herself and this stranger. Do everything she could to stop her soft heart from getting her killed and proving her mom's theory true.

Instead, she found herself asking, "Look, why don't you sit down? I'll get you some coffee."

Braden ran a hand over his face and shifted his weight. "You don't have to do that. That's not why I came. It's really not."

"I insist. I know someone who needs caffeine when I see him."

A hint of hope appeared in his gaze before quickly disappearing. "Only if you're sure. I can leave if I make you uncomfortable."

"I'm sure. Have a seat." Lisa wasn't actually sure. But she'd already put the offer out there. Now she hoped she didn't regret it.

Because today might not be as lucky as yesterday.

Before she could think about it too long, her phone buzzed just then. She looked down and saw that she'd gotten a message from her friend Wes.

Did U C this?

She clicked on the link he sent, which took her to a website. A message had been posted on the Facebook page for her restaurant.

Horrible food. Horrible service. Someone needs to close this place . . . permanently. It would be a favor to anyone who's ever thought about eating there. Anyone want to help me make that happen? Maybe we can run the owner out of town.

Lisa's stomach dropped. It wasn't that she was opposed to bad reviews. Well, she had to admit that she didn't like them. But she could sense the threat of danger in this one.

Had the same person who'd shot out her window left this?

She didn't know.

But a bad feeling loomed in her gut.

Chapter Five

LISA POURED Braden a hot cup of coffee, hoping she didn't regret inviting him to stay. She didn't want a repeat of yesterday.

Yet here they were.

Alone.

What if Braden snapped again?

Lisa shivered, trying not to second-guess herself so much. But as the memory of their first encounter jarred her thoughts, her arm jerked and coffee spilled onto the table.

She grabbed a napkin and tried to absorb the liquid before it dripped over onto Braden. "Sorry about that."

Braden grabbed some napkins and helped her soak up the coffee. "It's okay."

She gathered all the soggy napkins and tossed them into a nearby trashcan, willing herself not to act so nervous. *Get a grip, Lisa. Or ask him to leave. But don't waiver in this place of uncertainty.*

"Were you comfortable at Ty's last night?" She went to stand beside his table again, wondering if anyone else would come into her restaurant today. But that scathing review could have scared everyone away. After all, businesses lived and died by word of mouth. "Everything okay at the house?"

"It was fine." Braden shrugged, looking as if he wanted to say more as his hands hugged his coffee mug. But he didn't.

Braden took a long sip of his coffee, but life still didn't seem to be returning to him. This guy . . . he had some demons haunting him.

A pang of compassion rushed through Lisa. Not even Cyndi Lauper singing "Girls Just Wanna Have Fun" on her overhead could unearth Lisa's carefree side right now. She had too much on her mind. Mostly she was playing with the insane idea that this guy needed someone to help him, and she didn't see anyone else stepping up.

She jutted her hip out, decision made. She was going to help him. "Listen, how about some food? What can I get you?"

A flash of surprise shot through his gaze before he waved his hand in the air. "I don't want to impose. I really just came to apologize."

"Oh, you're not imposing. I'm charging you." Lisa grinned, trying to break the tension with some brevity.

A smile finally cracked Braden's face, and his shoulders relaxed some. "Okay then. How about an omelet?"

"I have a great one I make with pepperoni, sweet onions, and potatoes."

He raised his eyebrows, looking torn between being polite and being honest. "Could I just do bacon and cheese? I guess I'm not feeling very adventurous at the moment."

"One bacon and cheese omelet coming right up." Lisa got that reaction to her more creative recipes a lot, but foodies like herself loved the strange, innovative combinations that kept the taste buds guessing.

Lisa went back into the kitchen and kept one eye on Braden in the dining area as she cooked.

The man looked fairly normal as he sat there. But his shoulders seemed to carry an invisible weight. Why was that? And why did this man have her so curious? The best thing Lisa could do was forget about him and move on. Yet the curious, compassionate side of her couldn't do that.

Her gaze moved to the empty tables in her restaurant, and her stomach clenched.

No one else was here. If it wasn't the review, then it was probably the weather. The wind had picked up, and it was crazy cold outside today. Most locals were probably huddled inside, trying to stay warm.

This was the time of year when everyone hunkered down. Some people worked on restoring surfboards or crafting art or creating jewelry. Lisa usually spent the winter months whipping up new recipes and helping out with the local Meals on Wheels program.

Her phone rang, and Lisa saw that it was Tammy, her server. "Tammy, where are you? I've been calling all morning."

"I'm sorry, Lisa. I should have told you. But my friend Darlene and I decided to go on a road trip to Florida. We're in Key West right now, and we've decided to stay."

"For how long?"

"Indefinitely."

She bit back a harsh comment. "Some advance notice would have been helpful. I don't have anyone else to fill in for you. I'm by myself here today."

"Yeah, I'm really sorry. Good thing you're not busy at this time of year." Tammy didn't really sound all that sorry, which only grated on Lisa's nerves even more.

"Yeah, good thing."

How did someone forget something like telling her employer she was leaving for Key West?

Tension pressed in on Lisa as she slipped her phone into her back pocket. Great. What was she going to do now? Run this whole show by herself? She was already understaffed, and John's disparagements were still messing with her mind. All she needed was for people to add "bad service" to their list of critiques.

She knew she was overreacting to the negative analysis. If she was honest with herself, the insecurities probably went back to her childhood.

She'd always been the overweight one that kids had made fun of.

Until her junior year of high school. Then she'd decided to turn her life around. She'd started watching what she ate and exercising.

A year later, she was down forty pounds, and she'd managed to keep it off in the years since.

But deep inside, Lisa still felt like the overweight girl who didn't fit in. Who didn't feel good enough. Pretty enough.

That had been a long time ago, so why was she still holding on to those hurts?

She was a different person now, and one man wasn't going to ruin it for her.

Still turning the thoughts over, Lisa plated up Braden's omelet. The scent of eggs and cheese drifted upward, and she inhaled the aroma. The first part of enjoying food was seeing it. Then it was smelling it. And, finally, it was tasting it. That's what her grandmother had told her, at least, and her grandmother was the best cook she'd ever known.

She carried the plate over to Braden and placed it on the table. Against her better judgment, she sat down in the booth across from him.

"Looks great. Thank you." He bowed his head and said a quick prayer before digging in.

At least *that* was admirable. Had her first impression of the man been totally wrong? Lisa still wasn't sure.

But she wanted to find out.

"So tell me about yourself, Braden." Lisa rested her elbows on the table, determined to make the best of things.

"There's not much to tell." Braden lifted his fork, his arm trembling.

Lisa looked away, trying not to make him uncomfortable. But it was too late. He lowered his arm.

She hadn't intended on making him self-conscious. But she was curious about this man and what had really brought him here. Curious about the ghosts that haunted his gaze. Interested in what could have caused him to think she was a killer.

Keep talking, Lisa. Keep talking. "You had a secret job that's Special Forces without being a SEAL?"

"Yep, that's about right."

When he offered no more information, she asked, "Are you married?"

"Nope. Never have been. No kids."

She studied his face, trying to put together a mental analysis of him. He didn't seem to want to talk about himself, but she couldn't bring herself to blather on about inconsequential things like the weather or football. No, she wanted to know more about Braden. She needed to form a bigger picture of the man.

"How long have you been out of the military?"

"Two years."

"I guess you worked with Ty."

"On occasion." Braden absently rubbed his fingers against the side of his coffee mug. "We had some missions together and blew off some steam together when we were back in the States. He's a good guy."

There. He'd shared something more than an incomplete sentence. Her mission was done.

"Well, I hope you'll like it here. The weather is going to be a bear, though. A polar bear."

She cringed at her analogy. Her friends always said Lisa liked to do things her own way—both in the kitchen and in life. Yes, she marched to the beat of her own drummer. Some people got that and some people didn't.

Braden didn't even flinch at her corniness. "Polar bear or not—I'm not here for the beach. I'll be fine staying inside."

It took a special kind of person to be okay being alone. Most people Lisa knew preferred to fill up their days with busyness. It helped keep people's minds off their problems—even if it was just a temporary fix.

"Good timing then," Lisa finally said. "It's the perfect season for that."

Braden's gaze flickered to hers. "Look, I don't expect you to have anything else to do with me while I'm here. I'll look out for myself. I do appreciate the breakfast."

Lisa waved him off. "You're fine. Besides, I offered to cook for you. It's what I do."

A small part of her—a part that didn't make sense—felt a pang of worry for the man. While being alone could be an amazing chance to evaluate your life, it could also be a burden. She understood that. And something about this man screamed that he needed someone.

Braden pulled his gaze back up to hers. "Let me help you out here today."

Lisa blinked, uncertain if she'd heard correctly. "Help me out?"

"That's right. It looks like you're short-staffed. Besides, I heard you on the phone. Someone didn't show up to work, right?"

She frowned when she remembered her conversation with Tammy. "My waitress actually left town without any warning."

"So let me help."

"You don't have to do that." Lisa just couldn't see that working out, not with his issues—both his memory and the tremors in his hands. Forgetting customers' orders? Dropping their plates? It would be a recipe for disaster.

"I want to. I may not be able to do everything, but I can seat people. Take their orders. Refill their drinks—as long as the cups have tops on them."

As he said the words, a group of eight people stepped inside.

It *would* be nice to have some help. There was no way Lisa could handle this workday alone. And she didn't want to give critics any more ammunition.

Finally, she nodded and said with a semi-teasing tone to her voice, "Okay, but if you put any of my customers in a chokehold, you're out."

Braden smiled again and let out a soft chuckle. "It's a deal."

Lisa hoped that whatever this man was hiding didn't end up getting her in trouble.

Because he was definitely hiding something. She just had no idea what.

Chapter Six

BRADEN HAD COME out today for two reasons. The first was to apologize to Lisa. He honestly felt bad about what happened.

The second reason was because he needed to keep an eye open for trouble. Someone had set off those firecrackers. Had they done it to taunt him?

Braden didn't know yet. But he needed to find out. He needed to survey the area, see who was in town, and listen to the local scuttlebutt. And though he hadn't intended on volunteering to help Lisa, it was the perfect way to keep an eye and an ear on the town.

To Braden's surprise, he'd actually enjoyed helping out at the restaurant today. It hadn't been busy, but the people who'd come in had been interesting and mostly friendly. He'd found himself loosening up as the day went on.

Unfortunately, he hadn't seen any familiar faces. Nor had anyone given him a bad feeling in his gut. He had no more answers now than he had when he came here this morning.

He'd done okay as a server. He'd taken orders and delivered some food—the dishes he couldn't spill. It wasn't the ideal job for someone whose limbs quaked, but it had been doable.

As he bused a table, he stole a glance at Lisa from across the restaurant. She was talking near the breakfast bar with a customer, and her hands flew around in an animated fashion.

Braden hid a smile. The woman was surprising. She was just so bright-eyed and full of life.

So different from him.

And he was fascinated. He felt this crazy desire to learn more about her. To ask her how she came up with her crazy recipes. To figure out why she was still single.

Finally, at nine p.m., the last customer left, and Lisa flipped the sign to Closed. As she did, she leaned against the door, and an expression of delighted exhaustion captured her face. "Whew. That was busier than I expected. I guess it's a good thing you stayed."

"And I didn't put anyone in a chokehold."

She smiled, an action that screamed of sincerity and warmth. "That's right. It's a good thing you promised not to. Because the way Mr. Miller was talking about politics and religion, you may have wanted to."

Braden grinned again. What was it about Lisa that made him do that?

It was strange. In the past, before his injuries turned his dreams upside down, he'd dated beautiful women. Women who *knew* they were beautiful. Who spent hours making themselves attractive and who spent their entire paychecks buying only the best.

But Lisa was different.

She was beautiful in a natural way. And she was so down-to-earth. Just so . . . different. Braden couldn't put his finger on exactly what it was about her that he found so refreshing.

"Did you grab anything to eat when I told you to?" Lisa asked, moving away from the door toward the kitchen.

"I did. I had a grilled-cheese-and-peach sandwich with some of your homemade chips. It was delicious."

"That's one of my favorites." She paused for a second, absently straightening a pile of menus, and looked at him as if gathering her thoughts. "Listen, I just need to put a few things away and then I can drive you home. Sound okay?"

"Yeah, if you don't mind, I am a little tired." Ordinarily, it wouldn't have been a big deal. Or maybe Braden just liked the idea of spending more time with Lisa. Not that she would ever give him the time of the day—especially after the way he'd reacted to her yesterday. He knew she'd only let him help here at the restaurant today out of kindness. Or was it desperation?

"It's no problem. If you wouldn't mind putting the chairs on the tables, I'm going to grab the broom and sweep down the place. Then we can go."

As Braden began doing as she asked, he glanced up at Lisa again. "You mind if I ask a few questions about you?"

She paused from sweeping. "Me? Maybe. I can't promise I'll answer."

"How long have you lived here?"

"Three years. Came down from Ohio on a vacation and stayed. There's something about this place . . . once it becomes a part of you, you never want to leave."

Braden chuckled—one quick burst tinged with skepticism. "I'm not sure about that. I can't see a small town like this ever being appealing."

No, people liked to be in his business too much. He preferred to remain private, and small towns were no place for privacy. People there had nothing better to do than to talk.

"Anyway, I figure life is too short to live an existence that you don't love," Lisa continued.

Her words were absolutely true. He knew first-hand just how easily life could change. Anyone who'd been in the battlefield did. "I like that answer. Why'd you open this place?"

"Because I love combining food with science. It . . ." Lisa paused with the broom in her hands and looked off into the distance. "I used to work in a lab."

"Did you?"

"I did. Just call me your typical science geek. But coming here and doing this . . ." She shrugged. "I don't know. It brings me fulfillment. I had a job that paid great money but that left me feeling empty. It wasn't worth it."

"Kudos to you for making a positive life change."

She began sweeping beneath the booths again. "My turn to ask you more questions?"

Braden didn't have a warm and fuzzy story like Lisa did. And he wasn't able to give a straight answer about his career. There were so many mental holes everywhere else.

Still, he found himself saying, "Shoot."

"Why do your hands tremble sometimes?"

He sucked in a quick breath, tempted to blow her question off. But Lisa had been too kind to him to do that. "It's from a head injury."

Her motions slowed. "A head injury?"

"On the battlefield. It's . . . uh, well . . . it's caused some memory issues also, as you saw last night."

"Memories and trembles?"

He put the last chair up onto a table and leaned against the door frame. "Yeah, the doctors and my therapist don't quite know what to do with me. I'm a bit of an anomaly."

"I'm sorry to hear that. When Ty said you had a

disability, I thought . . . well, I didn't think that." Her cheeks reddened ever so slightly.

"Don't be embarrassed. Most people look at me and think I'm fine. And that's part of my problem."

Silence stretched between them until finally Lisa said, "Thanks for sharing that, by the way. I shouldn't have pried."

"It's really not a problem. I'm just starting to learn that it's okay to talk about it and not be ashamed."

Lisa swept the last of the crumbs into a dustpan and put the broom away. "I'll drive you back now. I have a few other things to do, but I can do them in the morning. I think we're both pretty tired."

"It's the good tired you feel after working hard." It certainly beat being alone and wrestling with his thoughts all day.

"Exactly. Let me grab my keys."

As Braden waited, he paced over to a framed article on the wall and read it. He smiled at the words there. The restaurant had been named one of the ten best in the state, with the reviewer calling the Crazy Chefette fun, innovative, and memorable, with tasty food and a warm staff.

He turned as Lisa joined him. "Nice write-up."

She smiled, though barely, almost like the article

made her sad. "Thanks. I was excited when I read it, and it brought a slew of customers this summer."

"You don't look very excited now."

She shrugged, still staring at the framed article. "I suppose it's just growing pains. There's one person in particular in town who doesn't like my place, and he's sure to let everyone know. It's become his personal mission to belittle me. I'm okay with the fact that not everyone will like me. But this goes beyond that. It's almost like the man has a vendetta against me."

"You can't let one person ruin your fun," Braden said.

As they walked outside, a brisk wind blew over them. Braden wished he'd brought a heavier coat with him. But he'd be fine.

He climbed into her sedan, feeling like a giant inside.

As Lisa glanced over at him, her eyes sparkled as if she could read his thoughts and agreed. "I guess cars like these weren't meant for men your size."

"My life feels like a circus, so maybe this is my clown-car moment."

She chuckled and took off into the dark night.

This was such a change of pace from Virginia

Beach, where he had been stationed. The roads there always seemed busy. On the other hand, the silence here on Lantern Beach was almost unnerving. Yet Braden wanted to be comfortable with the quiet. That was his goal. He needed the stillness to hear himself. To hear God. To heal.

At least, that had been his plan. Now, his survival instincts had kicked in as well. He had to be on guard. He would figure out who was trying to harm him, if it was the last thing he did.

A few minutes later, Lisa pulled to a stop at his temporary place.

"Thanks again, Lisa," he said.

It had been refreshing being around her today. Her world was totally different from his. Hers was filled with sugar and spice and everything nice. Filled with mentions in esteemed magazines. Filled with happy pumpkins placed strategically around her space, making everything festive and fun. His was filled with war and being forgotten by the very people he'd fought for.

"No, thank *you*," she said. "I don't know what I would have done without you."

Braden wanted to say more, but there was nothing else to say. Instead he nodded and climbed out.

But when he got to the top of the stairs, he froze. His front door was open.

Who had been here? Had it been the person trying to kill him?

And, if it was, where was this person now?

Chapter Seven

LISA HAD A SURPRISINGLY REFRESHING time with Braden today. He'd been a good worker. He had a nice smile—when he bothered to show it. And his massive presence made her feel surprisingly safe, which was most shocking when she considered their encounter the night before.

As she glanced at the passenger seat of her car, something caught her eye. Braden's phone. He must have accidentally left it when he got out.

Lisa grabbed the device and darted upstairs, hoping to catch him before he went inside.

She nearly collided with Braden at the top of the landing. He stood just inside the screened-in porch, staring at something in the distance.

Lisa peered beyond him and saw the front door was open.

"Braden?" she muttered, unable to figure out what was going on.

He stretched out his hand to stop her from getting closer.

"Stay here," he whispered.

Lisa took a step back, fear tightening her spine. No problem. She didn't want to go any farther. Especially not based on Braden's body language.

Was he just being paranoid again? Had his memory slipped, causing him to forget and leave the door open? It seemed like a possibility.

But what if that wasn't what happened and someone was inside?

Maybe she should call Austin or Wes for back up.

Or Mac.

Or . . .

Maybe Lisa should just pray.

Yes, pray.

That's what Lisa would do.

Dear Lord, I don't know what's going on here. But please keep Braden safe. And me too, for that matter.

She braced herself for whatever might happen

next. Was someone inside waiting? Would the intruder attack?

Or was this nothing? Another overreaction on Braden's part?

The questions pummeled her as time seemed to stand still around her. As Braden's phone buzzed in her hands, Lisa glanced at it. Without realizing what she was doing, Lisa read the text message that scrolled across his lock screen.

Do I need to warn you again?

Lisa sucked in a breath.

Do I need to warn you again? What did that mean? Was it a playful jab from a friend? Or was it ominous? A threat?

The words wouldn't leave her mind.

Braden was dangerous.

Or he'd brought danger with him.

Or . . .

She didn't know. But she didn't like this.

Finally, Braden lumbered out the front door, his gaze laser-focused on everything around him as he scanned the deck.

"Well?" Lisa asked, hugging her arms around her.

"Someone was inside." Braden's voice sounded

low and rumbling, easily matching his demeanor as he continued to scan his surroundings.

Inside? As in, someone had broken in? Any peace of mind drained from Lisa. "How do you know?"

He finally looked at her, all soldier and less disabled, yet still apologetic. "You'll see. And I don't know who. But no one is there now."

"Can I . . . can I look?" It was curiosity, Lisa supposed. The need to see what had happened. To see if Braden was exaggerating. But she had to know.

Braden nodded for her to go past. But Lisa only took one step through the doorway when she paused. Her eyes widened when she saw the mess inside. Someone had unmistakably been here.

Cushions were out of the couch. Cabinets were open. Chairs had been knocked over.

Nothing appeared destroyed. But still . . .

"We should call the police and report this," she muttered. "Just to cover all the bases."

Braden glanced around again and frowned, his hands going to his hips and reminding her a bit of a GI Joe figure with his strong jaw and steely gaze.

"Yeah, we probably should."

This had shaken Braden up. It was surprising,

considering Braden's size and background. He'd no doubt taken on terrorists, so he could definitely handle some mischievous kids who'd gotten bored.

Because that was most likely what had happened. In Lisa's estimation, at least.

Lisa pulled out her phone, hoping Mac might have some answers. But she had a feeling answers weren't going to be easy to find.

She only knew that someone was trying to send a message . . . a message she had no interest in hearing.

———

The police chief—Mac, Lisa had told him—drove up a few minutes later, his competent gaze showing years of experience.

"Thanks for coming," Braden said. "I'm Braden Dillinger."

Mac rubbed his snow-white goatee, looked around the great room, and shook his head with disgust. "No idea who did this?"

"No idea," Braden stood stoically beside Lisa.

"I'll take some fingerprints, but I doubt we'll find anything," Mac said. "It's confounding that nothing was taken. It's almost like someone was trying to send a message."

"I know it's probably a long shot, but since this is Ty's place, I thought we should report it," Braden said.

"It's a good idea," Mac said, turning toward Lisa. "After the incident at your place last night, I actually went to a break-in at a house not too far from here. One of the vacation rentals."

Braden stole a curious glance at Lisa. She hadn't told him about the incident at her place, and Braden wondered what that was about.

"Was anything taken?" Lisa asked Mac.

"The place was torn up and the copper wire was taken from the AC. But things like that happen around here at this time of the year. All of these deserted homes . . . petty thieves see a way to make some easy money."

"It's a shame," Braden said. "I guess I should check the outside unit?"

"I already did on my way up," Mac said. "It's fine."

"Why did someone go through the trouble of breaking into a home only to steal copper wire outside?" Braden asked.

It made no sense.

But there were other things that also didn't make any sense. Like the fact that someone was trying to kill Braden. Yet, for some reason, this person was drawing everything out. The person pursuing him already had the opportunity to kill Braden, yet he hadn't. Why not?

Were members of The Revolt trying to make their threats akin to water torture—slow and steady misery? If Braden's pursuer had found him, why not end it all and move on?

No, instead there had been the texts. The firecrackers. This break-in.

It didn't make sense.

"It's a good question," Mac said. "I suspect someone broke in looking for any valuables inside. When they couldn't find any, they went with Plan B."

"Well, I hope you find the person or people behind this," Lisa said. "People need some better hobbies when they get bored."

"Isn't that the truth?" Mac cast a glance at her, a fatherly look about him. "Keep me updated if anything else happens. And, in the meantime, keep your doors locked."

Braden shifted, heaviness still pressing on him. "I locked my door, Mac."

Mac paused. "Well, who has a key?"

"That's a question for Ty," Braden said.

"As far as I know, no one else besides me and Ty and Cassidy," Lisa said. "You know how protective Ty is of Cassidy. He's very careful."

Mac grunted again, his gaze far-off in thought. "I'd suggest changing the locks. And being very, very careful."

Braden intended on being just that. But he was also going to be proactive and find some answers.

Chapter Eight

WHEN MAC LEFT a few minutes later, Lisa turned to Braden. She knew she should go. She could sense the air of danger around Braden. Around his presence here on the island.

If she was smart, she would leave and never talk to him again.

Yet, she couldn't bring herself to do that. Perhaps she was too nurturing for her own good. She didn't know.

But she did find herself saying, "Let me help you clean up."

"You don't have to do that." Braden waved a hand at her. Was he anxious for her to get away also? Was that because he was hiding things from her—things that she didn't need to know because they weren't her business?

But ever since he'd arrived in town, nothing had been the same.

She took a step back, considering the wisdom of her actions. *Just leave, Lisa.*

But as Braden swooped down to pick up a dish, she saw his arms trembling again. The bowl clattered on the table as he placed it there.

Her heart softened, and her doubts seemed to melt away. "Don't be ridiculous. Two people will make half the work."

Before Braden could object again, she began putting the cushions back and picking up miscellaneous things around her. It didn't take long to put the house back together—less than twenty minutes.

When she put the last pillow in place, she turned to Braden, unable to ignore the questions that battered her. "You really have no idea who might have done this, Braden?"

He pressed his lips together for a moment and leaned against the breakfast bar. He stretched his arm out, balled his hands into fist, and frowned.

The tremors were worse than ever.

His shoulders seemed to slump. "No, I'm afraid I don't."

Lisa wanted to believe him. She really did. Yet she couldn't help but feel like there was more to this story. That there was a reason he'd put her in that chokehold. And that this place had been ransacked. And for that far-off, troubled look in his eyes.

She tilted her head and softened her voice before asking, "Why do I feel as if there's something you're not telling me."

Braden ran a hand over his face and stared into the distance. Finally, he looked at Lisa, a decision in his gaze. "Do you want to sit down?"

Lisa's curiosity flared to life. Would she finally get an explanation? Because the man had her full of questions. "Sure."

She lowered herself onto the couch, and Braden sat on the other end, a comfortable distance away.

He shifted uncomfortably as he seemed to wrestle with his thoughts. "I told you I have memory issues."

"You did."

He dragged his gaze up, a heaviness larger than Mt. Everest in his eyes. "You're going to think I'm crazy, but someone is trying to kill me."

Lisa blinked, certain she hadn't heard Braden correctly. Normal people didn't say things like that.

Then again, nothing about Braden seemed normal. "What? Who?"

"That's the problem." His jaw tightened. "I don't know. I can't remember."

Her thoughts raced ahead of her, trying to make sense of things. "You mean, like, a serial killer? Someone you made angry? Who would want to kill you?"

Braden's expression remained stoic—maybe even a little shocked or placid. "It's complicated, and the truth is, I just don't know. I only have my gut instinct."

Lisa shook her head, trying to comprehend that. "I . . . don't understand."

"In my job—"

"With Special Forces?"

"Yes. In my job with Special Forces, I made a lot of enemies. A lot of people have threatened to kill me. They've vowed revenge." He paused and shook his head.

"I see."

"Someone has been making threats. Watching me. Warning that they're going to strike soon. The problem is, I have no idea who is behind it. This person is faceless to me, which only makes them more dangerous."

Lisa's eyes widened. "I can't imagine."

"I'm not crazy."

"I didn't say you were." That explained why he'd put her in that chokehold. "Did you tell the police?"

"They can't do anything. I'm on my own. I hoped when I came here, I'd lose whoever is shadowing me. Apparently, that's not the case."

As she tried to process that, another question begged for her attention. "Braden, I know this is none of my business. But what happened to you? What caused your injuries?"

He glanced down, the past washing over him like a shadow.

Lisa slipped closer and placed her hand on Braden's arm. She felt the trembles beneath her fingers. But nearly as soon as she felt them, they were gone. They disappeared, almost like his muscles had flatlined.

Braden sucked in a breath. He'd noticed too.

Lisa pulled away, wondering if she'd overstepped her boundaries. It wasn't like she hadn't done that before—usually in the name of trying to help someone. Still, she'd be wise to keep her hands to herself right now.

"Listen, I don't know what happened," Lisa

continued, sitting on her hands. "And I don't know what you're going through. But I just wanted to say thank you for your service to the country. I'm sorry that this is what it did to you."

Braden's eyes caught hers, and something silent passed between them.

He stared at her, not saying a word for what felt like hours—hours that were probably only mere seconds. And then he looked away and drew in a deep breath.

"Thank you."

Lisa stood. She probably shouldn't have gone there. Shouldn't have touched him or asked so many questions.

She'd obviously made him uncomfortable. But, in a strange way, she'd seemed to calm him as well.

She cleared her throat, hating the tension tugging at her. "Okay, I'm going to go. I hope you get some sleep."

"I'll try." He stood also. "Oh, and Lisa?"

She paused halfway to the door.

"Why did you come back up here?"

Her cheeks flushed. "How could I have forgotten? You left your phone in my car."

She reached into her back pocket and pulled it

out. As she did, she remembered that text message she'd read there. *Do I need to warn you again?*

What had that meant?

It didn't matter.

It was none of her business.

Yet her gut told her there was more going on here than she could put her finger on.

Braden stared at his arms after Lisa left.

How had her touch managed to make his trembling stop? No one had ever managed that before. Nothing had.

The reaction was probably a fluke. And it didn't really matter. He most likely wouldn't see Lisa again, and there was even a less likely chance that she'd be touching his arm again—not after her knee-jerk reaction. She looked like she'd been burned.

The woman was fascinating to him. On one hand, she was cute and perky and passionate about her job.

On the other hand, she had a fire in her eyes and something a little broken about herself also.

He recognized it only because he felt it in himself so much.

There was something missing in her life as well. But what?

It didn't matter. Braden was only here for a week or two. He needed to find whoever was responsible for these threats on his life and move on. Even if he couldn't discover who the person was, he needed to remember that he would be moving on.

Island life was idyllic for many people. But not him.

He sighed and stood.

With Lisa's help, they'd tidied up the place. But he still needed to take out his trash. He gathered up the bag and took it downstairs to where a big black trashcan on wheels waited. He flipped on the overhead light and opened the top.

As he did, he paused.

What was that inside?

He reached into the depths of the canister and pulled something out. It was copper wiring.

What?

He remembered Mac's update on how someone had broken into a home last night and stolen this very thing.

But . . .

No, Braden had blacked out last night.

He hadn't broken into a house in the process.

An image of Ty's place hit him.

What if Braden was the one who'd ransacked it before leaving this morning?

No. He squeezed his eyes shut. Braden would remember something like that. He hadn't blacked out today . . . had he? He had drifted off to sleep on the couch this morning, but just for a few minutes, before he'd walked to the Crazy Chefette.

But that wouldn't make sense.

Braden rubbed his temples, feeling the start of a headache.

What was he supposed to do? Tell the police chief that he'd found this in his trashcan? Then the whole town would cast Braden in a suspicious light. He knew how small towns worked. And that would prove to be the opposite of what he wanted for this trip. He needed to relax, not be the object of scrutiny.

Whoever those thieves were, they must have disposed of the evidence here at his place. And maybe they'd set off those fireworks afterward. It was the only thing that made sense.

The only thing Braden didn't know was why. *Why* someone would do such a thing. Unless they were trying to set him up. But what sense would that make? He had far bigger issues in his life.

He'd have to think about that a little more. For now, Braden wanted to get back inside before he had any more episodes.

And there was one more thing he needed to do.

He went to his suitcase and opened it, reaching into a pocket for the gun he'd brought with him. It couldn't hurt to have it nearby, just in case trouble came this way.

But the compartment was empty.

What?

That couldn't be right.

He dug deeper.

No, his gun was definitely gone.

Wait. He'd taken it outside with him last night. And this morning, he'd awoken on the screened-in porch. He'd passed out.

But his gun hadn't been with him.

It didn't make sense. Where would it have gone? Had Braden done something with it? Or had someone stolen it?

He knew what the most likely answer was.

The bad feeling in his gut churned even harder.

Just what was someone planning for his future?

Chapter Nine

LISA RUSHED up the steps to her place, showered to get the scent of the restaurant off her, and then paused. Tea and a book might be calling, but she felt restless.

She couldn't bring herself to try and unwind. Not yet.

And she wasn't sure why.

Because of the scare at Ty's place? Because of being around Braden?

No, that wouldn't make sense.

Braden was . . . well, he was an enigma. Scary. Kind. Tough. Gentle.

She just wasn't sure yet which was the real Braden or if all those things could comprise a man.

Out of curiosity, she grabbed her laptop, sat on

the couch, and pulled up a search engine. She typed in "Brain Injury Tremors Memory Loss."

Numerous results came up.

Based on what she read, it appeared Braden had something called post-concussive syndrome. The symptoms included headaches, dizziness, mood swings, and difficulty remembering. Doctors generally treated the symptoms instead of the cause.

What about the tremors?

Nibbling on her bottom lip, Lisa kept reading. That could also be another symptom of brain injury.

Maybe that was why Braden's doctors and therapist said he was a unique case—or an anomaly as Braden had said.

She leaned back and processed that for a moment.

So Braden had gone off to war. Something had happened causing this head injury. He'd left his military career behind in order to heal. No doubt he'd been through therapy and counseling.

Had those things not worked?

That had left Braden coming here to Lantern Beach with hopes that the change in scenery could help.

Just then, a smattering of wind and rain hit the window, and Lisa startled.

It's just the weather, she told herself.

Still, she found herself replaying the window shattering last night. She wanted to believe it was just a bored teen playing a prank, but she knew that wasn't true. Someone had been trying to send her a message. They'd used a gun.

Perhaps that message had been deadly.

Shoving aside those thoughts, she continued with her online search. According to what she was reading, Braden's condition could last for days or weeks or months or, in some cases, even years.

A rock settled in her stomach at the thought.

It must be horrible living with that. Forgetting things.

Or would forgetting traumatic situations be a gift?

Lisa wasn't sure.

It was out of the tragedies that people learned. The hard parts of life strengthened a person's character. It taught people to appreciate the good and to be compassionate for others when they suffered.

Plus . . . not knowing was sometimes the hardest thing. It was better to face reality than to avoid it.

She closed the laptop and leaned back into her soft cushions.

None of this mattered. Braden would be here for a week or two. Then he'd be gone, and Lisa's life would resume.

It was best if she kept her distance, especially until she got a better feel for the man.

She only wished her brain got that message because she couldn't stop thinking about Braden.

She stood and paced toward the window, deciding she needed to stretch her muscles. As she glanced outside, she saw a shadowy figure standing there.

Her breath caught.

It was just a passerby who'd stopped on the sidewalk. Nothing to worry about.

But the man didn't leave.

The darkness made it hard to make out any details. Maybe the man wore a thick coat. He stood in the street, directly in front of her place.

And it almost appeared . . . like he was looking right at her.

Lisa stepped back, suddenly feeling like she was in a fishbowl. She was overreacting here. Too much had happened. It had her on edge.

But as she stole one more glance outside, she saw a flash.

Someone had taken a picture of her, she realized.

She slunk against the wall, hardly able to breath.

Who could it be? John Linksi? Braden? Or someone else entirely?

Wes, Austin, and Skye came into the Crazy Chefette the next morning after church, before the restaurant even opened. The gang tried to catch up with each other as much as possible, and lunch after church had become a tradition—for now. They also met on Thursday evenings for Bible study.

Lisa had fixed a bacon-and-egg lasagna, and everyone chowed down. The aroma of bacon and vanilla floated in the air, and the surprisingly sunny day made the moment feel nearly idyllic.

As they sat there, she glanced across the table at Skye and Austin and smiled.

Her friends, who'd just started officially dating about a month ago, looked oblivious to everything else around them. Austin took his napkin and dabbed the corner of Skye's mouth. She giggled and leaned close to say something.

Lisa looked away, her heart letting out a surprising ache at the sight.

"It's enough to make you sick, isn't it?" Wes mumbled beside her, nodding across the table toward their friends. "In a good way."

"Yeah, it is. First Ty and Cassidy, now Austin and Skye."

"You don't have to worry about me. I'll be single for a while."

"You're in no hurry, are you?"

He twisted his head in a quick no. "Not at all. I personally think the single life is the good life."

Lisa nibbled on her bottom lip, wishing she shared the sentiment. It would make her life so much less complicated. She shifted as she turned her thoughts away from her love life. "By the way, how's Kujo making out with Ty gone?"

Wes was taking care of the golden retriever while Ty was away.

"He keeps me on my toes. I've been taking lots of walks at the beach."

"Sounds romantic." Lisa smiled.

"Yeah, just what I always dreamed about." He rolled his eyes in a good-natured manner.

Austin turned away from Skye and back to the group discussion. "Speaking of Ty and Cassidy's absence . . . How's that guy who's staying at Hope House?"

Lisa drew in a deep breath, trying to figure out how to answer that. "Braden? He's . . . well, he's interesting."

"Interesting good or interesting bad?" Wes took a sip of his orange juice and waited.

"Well, he thought I was breaking in on the first night he got there, and I was afraid for a minute that he was going to kill me. That was fun." Lisa still shivered at the memory.

"Wow. That doesn't sound good." A knot formed on Wes's forehead.

"Nope, it wasn't. And I was ready to write him off. But then he came into the restaurant yesterday and gave me a token of apology. He also gave me a hand here, and he was different. I think he has some PTSD."

"Is it safe to be around him?" Austin asked, concern stretching through his voice. "You said you thought he was going to kill you. That's no joke. Is he unstable?"

"I guess as long as I don't surprise him it's okay." Lisa shrugged, wondering about the wisdom in her casual words. "I really don't know much about this. But I'm being careful. And I've already talked to Ty."

"Just be smart," Wes said. "And call us if you need anything. PTSD is nothing to play with."

Lisa glanced at the door and saw a figure there, peering inside. It was . . . Braden? Again?

"Speak of the devil," Lisa muttered. "I guess you'll all get the chance to meet him."

She unlocked the door, let him inside, and then locked it again. Braden looked a little better today, not quite as pale or disheveled as he had over the past couple of days. But his massive, overpowering frame still took her breath away at the sheer thought of what he was capable of.

No one in their right mind would want to be on the wrong side of this man.

"I wondered if you needed help again today." Braden looked beyond her and nodded at her friends. "But maybe you already have backup."

"These are my friends. We're just catching up before I open." Lisa shifted, pondering his words. Wondering about the wisdom of her choices. Questioning whether she was thinking with her heart more than her brain—something she'd been accused of more than once. "But you're here to relax. Coming to work here isn't exactly relaxing."

"I know. But I don't mind. In fact, yesterday was kind of fun."

Lisa stared at Braden, trying to gauge his sincerity. He definitely seemed serious. He wanted to help.

And he *had* done a decent job yesterday.

Her mind flashed through everything that had happened. A bullet shattering her window. A figure standing outside her house.

Braden wasn't responsible for any of those things. No, she'd seen his eyes. He wouldn't do that.

That first night they'd met, it had just been a misunderstanding.

"Okay, if you want to help, then I won't stop you. But the no chokehold rule still applies." She nodded across the restaurant. "Now, let me introduce you to my friends."

Chapter Ten

WORKING at the Crazy Chefette definitely beat spending the day alone at Ty's house. If Braden was going to find answers then he needed to get out and begin looking. A restaurant like this was one of the best places he could do that. Besides, maybe he could keep an eye on Lisa as well.

Braden hadn't gotten much sleep last night. No, he had too much to think about.

Mostly, he thought about that copper wire, and he wondered where it had come from. He thought about the house being broken into and wondered who was behind it. He thought about the strange texts and tried to figure out who might want to kill him. He wondered about what happened to his gun, and questioned if he should report it to the authorities. Probably.

Not being able to remember passages of time was such a curse. He hated questioning himself.

How much longer do I have to suffer with this, Father? I thought you would have delivered me by now.

"Order up!" Lisa yelled from the kitchen.

Braden walked to the window to grab the food. Some—involving soups or drinks or anything he could spill—Lisa had taken to delivering herself. But the plates and platters he could usually handle, though he did get some strange looks from a few patrons as his hands trembled.

He delivered the new batch of food, marveling again the combinations Lisa had come up with. She was brilliant and creative and warm—unlike anyone else he'd ever met, really. Who else would think to put together a hamburger with peanut butter? Or Rueben casserole? Or lemonade with jalapenos?

"You must be Braden."

Braden pivoted, ready to go on the offensive. He jerked his gaze toward the man sitting alone in a booth. Did he know this guy? He didn't think so.

Was he a member of The Revolt?

His gut told him no. But he had to be cautious.

The man seemed to read his tense reaction. "I'm Jack Wilson, the pastor at Ty's church. Former Navy chaplain."

Braden remembered that Ty had mentioned him. He stared at the man now, realizing that he'd envisioned a short, pudgy man. Instead, the pastor was probably his age—maybe a couple years older. He had curly blond hair that was messy but relatively short, and he wore a white linen shirt with the sleeves rolled up.

Nope, he definitely wasn't who Braden had pictured.

"That's right," Braden said. "Good to meet you."

Jack leaned back and picked up his coffee. "How's everything going for you here?"

Braden glanced around, saw no one was flagging him down or appeared to need any help, and turned back to Jack. "I'm getting through."

Jack's gaze scanned the restaurant. "By working here?"

"Work is good for the body and soul. That's what my dad always said."

"Sounds like a smart man." Jack leaned forward, his elbows on the table. "Look, if you need anything while you're in town, let me know. My place is right beside the church—the only one on the island. I'd be happy to offer a hand or a listening ear."

Braden remembered the copper wire again and felt like confessing. Not that Jack was a priest with a confessional or anything. But still, there was some kind of privacy that had to be adhered to as a pastor, right?

"I appreciate that. And I might take you up on the offer."

As Braden stepped away, his phone buzzed again. He took it out of his pocket and looked at the screen.

It was from the unknown number again.

Our plan is in place, and we've set up an additional target. After all, two are better than one. Right, Braden?

A picture was attached to the text. Braden waited for it to load onto his screen.

When it did, he sucked in a breath.

Lisa.

It was a picture of Lisa.

Retrieving something from the pantry. By herself. And, based on the clothes she wore in the photo, this was taken today.

Braden glanced around, but no one in the

restaurant looked his way or had their phones out. But this person who was tormenting him was close.

And now Lisa had been pulled into this mess.

His stomach clenched.

That was the last thing he wanted.

And now he had to figure out what he was going to do about it.

As the day wound down, Lisa realized just how tired she was. She was thankful that Braden was here to help because the customers had been steady. Braden had been surprisingly attentive to her guests again today, and there hadn't been any incidents.

She was only an hour from closing, which was good. She was ready to rest.

Lisa looked up from wiping down the breakfast bar counter as John Linksi stepped inside.

Her entire body tensed.

The man had obviously been drinking. His light blue T-shirt was stained with sweat or spilled alcohol or both. His steps staggered. His eyes were bloodshot.

Thankfully the last customer had just left. Maybe that would make this less humiliating because Lisa could sense the man was on a warpath.

Lisa felt rather than saw Braden come stand beside her.

"I need some *foie gras*," John announced, stumbling toward Lisa.

Lisa could smell the beer and cigarettes on him. She could sense the way he'd lost his inhibitions. The man probably wasn't much older than she was, yet he appeared decades older. Maybe it was the drinking or the unknown tragedy that had happened to him.

She had no idea.

"We don't have any foie gras." She kept her voice firm and steady. If there was one thing she knew about drunks, it was that she couldn't entertain them. No, her boundaries needed to be clear.

"Then make me some." John stopped in front of her and met her gaze head on.

"I don't do custom orders. Sorry."

"Well, this is a sorry restaurant then. What kind of place doesn't have foie gras? I'll tell you what kind. A *weird* restaurant. And that's what this joint is. Weird. Everyone around town thinks so. It's a weird restaurant run by a weird wannabe cook. Or, should I say, chef?" John laughed obnoxiously loud. "Like anyone believes that."

Lisa's cheeks warmed with embarrassment. Of course John had to make this personal and insulting. But instead of cowering, she raised her chin higher.

Braden started to speak, but Lisa raised a hand to stop him. She wasn't ready for him to step in. Not yet.

"We're closing," she said. "You need to leave. Now."

John leered closer, his unseemly stench overwhelmingly bad.

"I don't want to leave. I want foie gras." Even though his voice grew louder, his words still slurred.

Lisa crossed her arms. "And I told you, we don't have any."

"Well, what *do* you have?" His eyes skimmed lower, and a suggestive smile crossed his lips.

The next instant, John flew back.

Braden appeared in front of Lisa, his broad chest acting as a shield and separating her from danger. Adrenaline seemed to pulsate from him.

"You heard the lady," Braden growled. "She wants you to leave."

John scrambled to his feet, but the alcohol in him apparently made him braver than usual. "You don't own this place, and you can't tell me what to do."

"You want to try me?" Braden rolled his shoulders back, making him appear even larger.

Lisa held her breath, watching as the two men faced off.

She only hoped this didn't turn any uglier than it already was.

Chapter Eleven

LISA FELT Braden nudge her behind him as he faced off with John.

"Maybe I do want to try you." The drunk man stared back at Braden, spittle clinging to his chin. His thinning brown hair stood up and appeared greasy. Lines stretched at his forehead and eyes.

This man was a walking disaster.

Braden's hands went to his hips, and his chest broadened, making him even more imposing. "I'd rather do things the easy way. For your sake."

Anyone should be afraid of Braden right now. He was big, strong, and unwavering.

And Lisa was so glad she was on this side of him. To his back. Protected. Safe.

"I'm just a lonely man who needs some food

and company," John continued, his voice deflating slightly. "You can't blame a guy for that."

"That's not what I'm blaming you for." Braden glowered. "I'm blaming you for acting like a jerk. Now get out of here before things turn ugly."

John stared at Braden a moment longer before taking a step back and nodding. "Fine. I'm out of here. Never liked this place anyway."

Braden didn't move until John was out the door and out of sight. Then he turned toward Lisa with concern in his warm brown eyes.

"You okay?" He studied her expression.

Lisa nodded and looped her hair behind her ear, feeling shaken—both from the encounter and from Braden's attention. "Yeah, I'm fine. I'm just glad you were here."

"I'm glad I was also. What a jerk."

She tried to brush off the encounter. But she also needed to get away from Braden because she'd been staring at his muscles a little more than she should have been. Braden might be broken, but he was still dangerous.

That also meant he was off-limits.

"John is like a tick around here," Lisa finally said. "He sucks the life out of everyone, passes on diseases, and gives nothing in return."

"Ouch. Yeah, he seems like a leech." Braden stooped lower, still appearing concerned. "You sure you're good?"

"I'm fine." Lisa's cheeks heated at his attention.

"Maybe I should walk you home tonight, just to be on the safe side."

"Well, you could. But I live upstairs, so it would be a short walk."

Braden grinned—the action just a brief flash—before shoving his hands into his pockets. "I guess it would. At least I know you'll be safe, though."

Something stretched between them a moment. Lisa wasn't sure what. She only knew that her first impression of Braden was turning out to be wrong.

And that fact, for some reason, delighted her entirely more than it should.

Off-limits, she reminded herself. Off-limits.

Just as Braden stepped outside to head home, a police cruiser pulled into the lot.

His back muscles tightened as he waited for what would happen next. Mac stepped out and sauntered over toward him. Just as he did, Lisa stepped outside, concern etched onto her face.

"I saw you pull up," she said, pulling her sweater closer. "Is everything okay?"

"There was another break-in last night, not far from where you're staying, Braden," Mac said. "More copper wire was stolen. We still don't have any leads."

Braden felt the blood drain from his face but tried not to show it. "That's a shame people are that bored."

"I agree. We don't have any leads as to who broke into Ty's place yet, either. But we're working on it."

Braden hadn't done it. He couldn't have. Wouldn't have. So why did he feel guilty? And, even worse, where was his gun?

"Is that why you stopped by, Mac?" Lisa shifted her weight, turning against the wind.

Mac shook his head. "I just thought I'd ask you to keep an ear open. You know how chatty people can be while they're eating. If you hear anything, let me know. This little crime ring is getting on my last nerve. If I ever want Cassidy to ask me to fill in again, I need to put the kibosh on it."

"Absolutely," Lisa said. "No word on my broken window either?"

"Not yet. But we're still investigating."

Broken window? It was the second time he'd heard her mention an incident—and he'd seen the broken pane on her back door. Some kid must have gotten bored and thrown a rock through it or something.

Braden watched as the chief climbed into his cruiser. With one more glance and nod back at Lisa, Braden started his walk home.

His thoughts undulated between everything that had happened since he'd arrived in town. But mostly, he thought about Lisa.

He was glad he'd been there when that man had come in. The thought of anyone hurting Lisa . . . it sent fire up his spine. She'd handled herself pretty well, but the man had been aggressive. Was he the one who'd been upsetting her with his insults as of late?

It was strange that Braden felt so attracted to Lisa. His feelings were unlike anything he'd experienced before. Stronger than they should be. They preoccupied his thoughts and put a new bounce in his step. But until he figured himself out, there was no room in his life for a relationship of any sort.

Not that Lisa would ever be interested in dating him. No, she seemed pure, like a piece of fresh fruit from a pristine farm. Braden, on the other hand, was the piece of fallen and bruised fruit from soil that had been over-farmed and sprayed with too many pesticides.

He walked up the driveway to Ty's place and paused at the trashcan. He held his breath a moment as he stared at it.

There's nothing inside it, Braden told himself. No, he'd removed the copper wire he'd found earlier and put it in the shed beneath the house. He'd figure out what to do with it later.

And Braden hadn't blacked out last night . . . he didn't think so, at least. So all of his anxiety was for nothing. It was unfounded.

Still, he hesitated as he reached for the lid. He nudged it open and peered inside. His stomach sank when he saw the wires there.

What in the world . . . ?

Was he really behind the break-ins? If not, how had these gotten here?

Chapter Twelve

LISA HAD DECIDED that Mondays were her days to experiment with new recipes—right after she did a few chores around the restaurant. She was surprised as she finished mopping the floors after lunch to look up and see Braden at the door. A flutter of delight swept through her.

Leaning the mop against the counter, she walked toward him and twisted the lock. As the door opened, a strong wind swept inside. The chill it brought with it matched the gray, gloomy day outside.

"Closed today?" Braden asked, rubbing his hands together.

"I am. Watch out for the wet floor. I'm doing a

little deep cleaning and playing with some recipes. Sounds fun, huh?"

He shrugged, as if the idea didn't totally appall him. "You need help?"

She jutted her hip out and stared at him, trying to read his body language. "You're really not good at this not working thing, are you?"

Braden shrugged. "No, I'm not good at it at all."

Lisa stared at him a moment, trying to decide her response. Her first instinct was to try and get rid of the man. But another part of her thought the company could be fun. Braden had been different yesterday and the day before. Maybe that was the Braden Ty knew and what happened the first day Lisa met Braden was just a fluke.

"If you're just trying to make up for that first night, then I should let you know, your debt is paid," she told him. "No worries."

He offered a half shrug. "I still do feel bad about that. But I actually kind of like it here. I've never been good at not doing anything."

"I can understand that." Lisa released her breath. "Look, if you'd like to help me out, feel free. The pay isn't great. It's just dinner."

"It sounds like a winner to me."

Easy-to-please people were sometimes refreshing. "Let's get busy then. You ever replaced a window?"

"Actually, I have."

"Great. Mine got shot out earlier this week."

Braden stopped in his tracks, and his face looked pale. "What? I heard you say your window was broken but . . . someone shot it?"

She nodded. "It happened a couple of nights ago. Someone just came past, fired the window out, and left."

"No idea who? Or why?"

"Not a clue. I'm hoping it was just someone who got bored and had nothing better to do. It beats the other possibilities."

"For a sleepy little island, there sure does seem to be a lot happening around here lately."

"Yeah, you're right. There does." She nodded toward a storage room in the back. "I have all the supplies I need. My friend Austin stopped by and dropped them off. He said he would come back tomorrow to fix it. He's apparently in the middle of a big job right now, and I didn't want him to stop. So, if you could do it, that would be awesome."

Braden followed her to the back, beyond the kitchen. She showed him everything he would need to replace the pane, and he wasted no time getting started. She lingered close by, sitting on one of the steps leading to her apartment, in case he needed help.

Lisa cleared her throat. She wasn't one for silence—not if there were things to talk about, at least. "So, do you like Lantern Beach so far?"

Braden pulled the wooden patch from her door and examined the broken pane. "It's beautiful. No one can deny that."

But small-town living wasn't for him, Lisa reminded herself. It was better that way and a good reminder that she should keep her distance. After all, Braden wasn't dangerous, but he also wasn't permanent around here. There was no need to grow too close to the man.

He brushed out the remaining shards of glass. "Tell me about Ty's wife. She must be pretty special."

"Cassidy? Oh, she's really great. She's dedicated and loyal and smart, not to mention beautiful. She just took over as police chief, and she's doing a great job. It makes a big difference when someone cares about the area." Lisa grabbed the broom and dustpan and swept up the stray glass.

"I can imagine."

She glanced at Braden as he used a putty knife to scrape around the edges of the empty pane. He was the hotshot soldier doing menial household tasks—but he'd never once complained about it either. Lisa was impressed.

She folded her arms across her chest and watched him. "What do you do, Braden? I know you were in the military, but are you working anywhere now?"

"No, I'm just in recovery mode." A certain sadness tinged his voice.

"Any plans for after recovery mode is finished?"

"I've thought about that a lot. And I don't know for sure. A lot of people who leave the military go into law enforcement or private security. I'm just not sure that's for me. Not in my current mental state, for sure."

"Well, the Lantern Beach PD is looking to hire someone." She wasn't sure where the suggestion had come from, but it seemed like an idea she should throw out.

"Is that right?" He chuckled as if the idea were absurd as he picked up the pane of replacement glass Austin had gotten her.

"What?" Lisa put a hand on her hip. "You can't see yourself hanging around here?"

"No, actually, this place would be like having shore duty. There's not much excitement in it." Carefully, he placed the new glass in the window and pressed the putty knife into it, using some kind of compound to hold it into place.

"So you liked deployment?" Was he the type who always liked to leave? Who thrived on adventure instead of routine? On fleeting relationships instead of settled ones?

He didn't turn his gaze away from the door. "It was exciting. But you learn to live off adrenaline. That doesn't bode too well for everyday life."

"I can imagine."

A few minutes later, Braden stepped back and looked at his work. "All done. You might just need to touch up the paint."

She stood and inspected the door. "Looks good. Thank you for doing that."

He wiped his hands with a rag as he turned toward her. "Now what?"

Someone who was ready to work. Lisa liked that. "Now for the fun part."

"Fun part? That wasn't fun?"

"Well, it *was* satisfying." Lisa led him to the kitchen. "But we should have some coffee."

"I can handle that. Let me just wash up first."

As he did that, Lisa reached over the counter and grabbed a coffee mug. She filled it, mixed some special ingredients into it, and handed it to Braden. "Part one of my experiment. The coffee. What do you think?"

"Experiment, huh?" Braden took a sip and almost spit it out. "What is this?"

She grinned as she turned on her favorite mix of cooking music. "Candy Man" began to play.

"It's coffee," she said, feeling the glimmer in her eyes. "Of course."

"With?"

"Cayenne and coconut milk. Try it again. It needs to grow on you."

"I have no words." He raised the mug, as if contemplating what to do next.

"Just one more sip?"

"I'll feel emasculated if I say no." Braden raised the mug higher and rolled his neck before taking another drink. "Okay, the second sip was better. Now that I know what to expect."

"Cayenne pepper promotes excellent cleansing properties within our internal systems, and it helps your metabolism rev up. The coconut milk is a little healthier than half and half. But I'm still playing with various ideas."

His gaze caught hers. "I think you're brilliant, Lisa."

Her heart lifted with delight before she looked away, her cheeks burning. Was there more to the look in his eyes than a mere compliment? Or was Lisa reading too much into things? And why did one part of her like his affirmation?

She cleared her throat and turned back to her work station. "But the really fun part is my experiment with apple pie."

"Sounds intriguing. I love apple pie."

"Thanksgiving is right around the corner, and I plan on having all of my friends plus a few others over to the restaurant to celebrate. They're expecting something with my creative twist."

"I can only imagine they are."

She turned toward the pie dishes that she'd already laid out. "I have three different kinds of apple pies I want to make. I want to see which one tastes better. You can help by being my taste tester."

Braden leaned against the counter, his bulky arms crossed over his chest. He looked more relaxed than she'd ever seen him. "What are these pies? And why mess with a classic?"

"Because if you settle for what's always been

good enough then you never know what could be better."

His gaze caught hers. "I like that."

"Good." Lisa's heart pounded in her ears as she looked up at him.

Braden put his coffee down. "Okay. Teach me your ways, oh great one."

"All right, there are the three pies we're making." Lisa began ticking them off on her fingers. "One is a rustic apple pie made with a cornmeal crust."

His face almost looked comical as he tried to hold back his disgust. "I'm not judging you. I'm really not."

"Another is a cheesecake apple pie."

"I could dig that."

"With rosemary," she added, flicking her finger in the air as if it were a magic wand.

He twisted his head with doubt. "You're starting to lose me just a little."

Lisa pushed ahead before he lost interest. "And the third is an apple tart, but I peel the apples so they look like roses."

Braden made a face.

"And I add bacon."

"I'm back on board."

She hid a smile. "You're going to make the crusts for me."

Lisa grabbed the ingredients he'd need and placed them on the counter.

"Never made crust," Braden admitted.

"It's easy. I'll teach you." She grabbed a large mixing bowl, some measuring cups, and spoons.

"Would you?"

"Absolutely. But you might have to get your hands dirty." She wiggled her fingers in the air.

"I'm not afraid." He winked.

Lisa raised her eyebrows. "You should be."

Braden chuckled, seeming less like a soldier and more like a teddy bear. She liked both sides of him —as long as she was on the right side of him.

"I'm up for the challenge," he said.

"All right, let's get started." She grabbed a huge bowl of apples that she would clean and slice. "First off, mix the cornmeal and sugar. Here's the recipe."

She placed the hand-written card in front of him and watched as he measured everything out.

"After you stir that, I'll cut in the butter."

"Yes, ma'am."

She leaned closer—maybe too close. She was close enough to smell his musky aftershave mixing with the scents of the food around them. Close enough that the hair on his arms brushed against her skin, sending delight prickling through her.

Braden was a good student and did as she asked. She worked the mixture until it formed crumbs and reached the perfect texture. "Now just roll it into a ball."

Braden tried to make a ball, but the mixture continued to fall apart. Lisa stood back and watched in amusement for a moment until she couldn't take it any longer. It was almost painful to see him struggle.

"Here, let me help you." She stepped beside Braden, took one of his hands, and showed him how to properly form the dough. "Just like this. You'll get the hang of it."

She sucked in a breath as a realization hit her. His hands had stopped trembling.

Again.

Braden must have noticed it also, and his eyes widened with a hint of awe. "You have the magic touch."

"I don't know about that." Lisa let out a nervous laugh.

She looked away before Braden read too much into the moment. Before he could read the look in her eyes or know that she'd felt a jolt of electricity herself. The last thing she needed was to fall for someone who wasn't in the right mental state.

"Okay, now what?" Braden's voice sounded strained as he asked the question.

She grabbed a handful of flour and splattered it on the stainless-steel countertop. "Now we roll it out."

Braden reached across her and picked up the rolling pin. "So tell me, Lisa, how did you become a scientist?"

She shrugged, stepping back to watch him as he began rolling out the dough. "Science was always my thing. I loved it. But I was working in the lab, creating . . . well, I was creating cosmetics. Long-lasting lipstick, for that matter. It just wasn't fulfilling, if you know what I mean."

"I get that."

"But what I'd always loved was to cook. Food is . . . well, it's more than a necessity. It's fun and a way to bring people together and a way to express myself." As she talked, she began preparing the apples.

"Interesting."

"My friends were always commenting on how much they liked it when I had them over to eat. Everything just kind of grew from that."

"It's good that you're doing what you love."

"I agree."

Just then, a rattle sounded in the distance. Lisa startled and took a step back. Was that someone trying to get in? The sign on the door clearly said the restaurant was closed.

"Stay here." Braden stiffened and snapped into bodyguard mode. "Let me check it out."

Lisa nodded, grateful Braden was here. Because what if it was another stray bullet? Or John was back? Or the man who'd been watching outside her place, who took a picture?

Facing those challenges with someone else beside her was way better than facing them alone—especially when that someone was Braden.

Chapter Thirteen

BRADEN WALKED TOWARD THE DOOR, his muscles on guard as he prepared himself for the worst.

But when he reached the front, he saw no one, nothing.

He stepped outside, just to be sure.

The parking lot was both dark and empty.

Strange.

What if the man who wanted to harm Braden was out here? But it wasn't just Braden he wanted to harm, Braden reminded himself. The man was now targeting Lisa also.

If something happened to her because of him . . . he'd never forgive himself.

Should he tell her about the photo and the threats?

No, he decided. It would only make her paranoid.

Instead, he'd try to stay close and keep an eye on her himself.

When he was certain nothing was awry, he joined Lisa again in the kitchen. But he still didn't feel at peace. They'd both heard something, and they were both in danger.

"Well?" Lisa stood against the wall, her eyes as wide as saucers as she stared at the door, as if she'd been waiting for him.

She was frightened. Maybe a little too frightened. While the rattling had been unnerving, the woman's reaction seemed bigger than what had happened.

Was there something he didn't know? Did this go back to that bullet that had gone through her window?

"Maybe it was the wind."

She released her breath and nodded. "Okay, good."

"Why do you look scared? You think someone is coming after you or something?"

"Not really. It's just that between someone

shooting out my door and John . . . I guess I'm
on edge."

Braden stepped closer and squeezed her shoulder. "I guess you are. I'm sorry, Lisa."

"Don't be sorry. It's not your fault. It's just got
me unnerved."

They stared at each other a minute, neither
saying anything.

Braden wanted to say more. Wanted to fish all
the secrets from her so he could understand her
better. But that wasn't his place.

They spent the next hour making the other
pies and munching on some sandwiches that
Braden made them. When everything was in the
oven, Lisa leaned against the counter, inhaling
deeply. She was a beauty with her dancing,
mischievous eyes and a rakish grin that promised
fun and heart.

"They smell good, don't they?" She raised her
eyebrows.

"Apples and cinnamon and sugar. Has there
ever been a better combination? I can hardly wait
to try them."

"Can I tell you something, Braden?" Lisa
crossed her arms and studied him a minute.

"Of course." His heart rate ratcheted up a

notch. Was this one of the secrets he could glimpse beneath the cheerful undercurrents of her gaze?

She pulled herself up on the counter, looking more laid-back and relaxed than she had a few minutes earlier. "I used to be overweight."

"I would have never guessed." She seemed naturally slender. Either way—slender or over-weight—Lisa was a beauty. He hoped she knew that.

"I decided to change my life. I was tired of being the fat girl, so I lost forty pounds."

"Good for you. That takes a lot of willpower."

"I did it by changing my thinking. Trying to use mind over matter."

"What do you mean?" Braden leaned back, interested in hearing what she had to say.

Her hands flew in the air as she talked, bringing the story to life. "Well, so many of our reactions are based on our thoughts and our core beliefs. My core belief was that food made me happy and brought me comfort."

"But . . ."

"I had to start looking at food as a necessity instead. Don't get me wrong. As you can tell with my job, I still find a *lot* of joy in food. But I filter that enjoyment through mental reminders to myself about why I do what I do."

"That's interesting." He believed in the power of the mind as well. It was too bad his wasn't working properly.

"It is. It goes back to discovering the lies that we've allowed ourselves to believe. After a while, those lies feel so much like the truth that we believe them and they become a part of us."

"It takes a lot of self-control." Braden stood from his perch against the counter. Lisa's attitude toward life and her determination were just more reasons why she was amazing. "I know this sounds like a line, and I don't mean it that way. I really don't. But why are you single?"

Lisa shrugged, looking surprisingly unaffected by the question. "I haven't found the right person, which also sounds cliché. But it's true. I don't want to settle."

"Admirable."

Her gaze met his. "You?"

Braden shrugged this time. "I was deployed. Not in a good place for a long-term relationship. And then I felt broken."

"We're all broken in our own ways, aren't we?"

"Even you?"

"Even me." She offered a soft smile. "It's weird, you know. I've always wanted to be married and have kids. All of my friends in college talked about women's rights and careers and being independent. I was a bit of an outcast. I wanted a career—but not like they did. I wanted a family more."

"That doesn't sound weird."

"Well, sometimes I think God has a wicked sense of humor."

"Are you allowed to say that?"

She shrugged. "I don't know. Am I? Okay, He has a strange sense of humor."

"Why is that?"

She sucked on her bottom lip. "The truth is— and I'm not ashamed of this—but the truth is that, out of all my friends, I'm the one who always wanted to settle down. And you know what's so ironic? I've never even been kissed."

Braden sucked in a breath, certain he hadn't heard her correctly. "What? You're joking with me."

"I'm not."

"Are you one of those people who's waiting for her wedding for her first kiss?"

"No, I'm just waiting for someone I honestly like. Who sees me for me. Who likes me for me."

"And you've never met someone like that? I

mean, you're pretty and smart and successful. There are probably guys waiting in line to date you."

She shrugged. "There have been a couple of guys who tried, but I wasn't interested. Truthfully, I may have lost weight, but part of me still feels like that overweight girl. I was always everyone's friend, the sidekick, but never the star of the show, if you get my drift."

"I find that hard to believe." Braden stepped closer so he could see Lisa's face, so he could study her eyes and see the flecks in them. "You're not the supporting cast character kind of girl. You definitely deserve your own story, Lisa."

Lisa raised a shoulder, but her expression didn't show embarrassment. No, she looked like she took it all in stride. "I'm as single as they come."

Was there anything this woman *didn't* take in stride?

It was an impressive trait to possess.

"Truth be told, I can understand." Braden's throat burned as he contemplated the wisdom in sharing his deepest thoughts. But something about Lisa made him want to open up. "I used to revel in my own toughness. And . . . now I hardly feel like a man anymore. What kind of a man can't even button up his own shirt?"

Her hand reached out until it rested on his shoulder. "I think when a guy truly acknowledges who he is, that's the manliest thing of all."

Warmth spread through him. She got him. Lisa really got him. There weren't any hints of pity in her voice. No, she understood.

There were so few people he could say that about. "Thanks for listening, Lisa."

"No problem," she said softly. "And you'll get there again, Braden. Just give yourself time."

"I wish I felt that sure."

She sucked in a deep breath, as if the moment overwhelmed her. Or was it because he'd stepped closer? Or because she'd realized her hand was on Braden's chest as they faced each other.

Braden half expected her to run. Instead, she picked up some flour from the canister beside her—just a small coating on her hand—and blew on it.

A cloud filled the air.

"Magic cooking dust." She grinned.

Braden smiled in return and grabbed some flour also. "I like that."

He blew some in her face until both of them were covered in flour and laughing.

Before either realized what was happening, Braden put one arm at each side of Lisa's hips as she sat on the counter. He moved in closer, a new emotion coming over him. A serious emotion.

"What would you say if I told you I wanted to kiss you right now?" His voice sounded so low that he wasn't sure Lisa would hear.

Lisa's pupils dilated. "I might be open to it."

One hand stayed at her waist and the other pushed a hair from her face. Braden's thumb skimmed her jaw as he soaked in her features. Her beautiful features. Features that highlighted her inner beauty.

What was he doing?

Braden didn't know.

But he did know that he didn't want to stop.

Chapter Fourteen

LISA CLOSED her eyes and breathed in the moment. The sweet smell of the pies baking. The feel of flour across her skin. The memory of Braden's lips against hers. Of his nearness. Of the musky scent of his cologne and the warmth of his skin and—well, everything. Everything about the moment was perfect.

"You sure you've never done this before?" Braden murmured, his breath wisping across her cheek.

"I'm quite certain." Lisa opened her eyes, and her cheeks warmed as she saw Braden watching her. It wasn't embarrassment. No, it was because all her emotions felt so big and unbelievably blissful inside her.

"You could have fooled me." Braden's gaze looked as warm and enticing as caramel syrup as he stared at her.

"You know what I think?" Lisa licked her lips, feeling electricity crackling in the air.

"What's that?"

"That you should stop talking and kiss me again."

A slow, warm smile spread across Braden's face. "I can do that."

His lips met hers again, just as tender as the first time. Lisa reached up and let her hands explore his jaw. The side of his face. The nape of his neck.

When they pulled away, she had to catch her breath. Her heart raced so quickly it almost felt unhealthy. Yet she'd never felt more alive.

"What are we doing?" Braden touched his forehead against hers.

"That's a good question." Lisa's heart warmed at his vulnerability. Nothing was more appealing than a man who wasn't afraid to be authentic. She'd never thought when she met Braden that he would be that man. Now the thought wouldn't leave her mind.

"I didn't come here looking for this." His voice

sounded mellow with emotion. "And now . . . well, I don't know how I'll ever walk away."

Lisa rested her hand against his jaw and cheek, feeling the stubble beneath her fingers. Now that he mentioned it . . . she thought the same thing. "Maybe you don't have to."

Something silent passed between them. Before either could say anything else, the oven timer dinged.

Lisa swallowed hard and pulled back. "The pies are ready. I know the perfect place to try them out."

"I'm game."

"Great. Let me get everything ready. You're going to love it."

While Braden carried a tray laden with their slices of pie to sample—along with a healthy serving of ice cream and two travel mugs with coffee—Lisa led him upstairs. She bypassed her small apartment and hit another stairway that led up even higher.

"Where are you taking me?" Braden asked, his eyes sparkling with curiosity.

Lisa smiled and held her lantern up so they could see. This part of the building didn't have any lights, which was part of its intrigue. "You'll see. Are you scared?"

"Scared? Do you think that's why I'm trembling?"

She smiled, glad he could laugh at himself. "Well, whatever you do, don't drop the pies."

Braden chuckled. "I like your humor."

She stopped at the top of the stairway and pushed up a hatch. Carefully climbing through, she put the lantern in the corner and took the tray from Braden. "Here we are."

Braden climbed up behind her and glanced around. "What is this?"

Satisfaction spread through her chest as she glanced around the enclosed space. "It's an old widow's walk."

"No way."

"Way. Isn't it cool? It's my favorite place ever."

Braden caught her gaze. "And you're sharing it with me? I'm honored."

Lisa shut the hatch. She kept blankets and over-sized pillows against one side of the space—the side that faced ocean. After they settled there, she lit a couple of candles and turned off the lantern.

"This really is incredible, Lisa," Braden said, staring out the window at the dark sky outside.

"I know, isn't it? You can see the stars. The moon. The ocean. I like to come here when I need to think."

"I can see why."

She swallowed the lump in her throat and reached for the tray. "Shall we try some of these creations?"

"Yes, let's."

They sampled each of the three pies, doing their best to impersonate the snooty judges from all of those on-screen cooking competitions. In the end, they decided the apple pie made with cornmeal crust won.

With full bellies, they leaned back into the pillows and stared out at the ocean.

"That was really fun, Lisa," Braden said.

"I'm glad you had a good time."

He rested his hand on her knee. Lisa leaned closer and took his hand, feeling surprisingly comfortable. Instead of holding it, she glanced at his palm and began tracing the lines there.

How was it possible that she felt this deeply, and so quickly at that? Was she setting herself up for failure and regret? She wasn't sure. Their relationship felt like treading unfamiliar—but thrilling—

waters. In fact, she felt as giddy as a girl with a crush.

"So, I asked earlier what you were going to do with your future," she started. "You really don't know?"

Braden took a sip of his coffee, but a new somberness came over him. "No, I don't. I know it sounds strange, but I feel like I've been swallowed by this hole that I can't get out of, no matter how hard I try or push myself."

"I'm sorry, Braden. I can't imagine how difficult that must be."

"Truth is, all the jobs I'm interested in, I'm not sure I'm cut out for." He shook his head slowly, his gaze still fixated out the window. "I just don't really know who I am anymore."

"You really think someone is trying to kill you?" Lisa asked.

He frowned and lowered his head. "Yeah, I do."

"Why? And who?" Lisa tried to put it together, to make sense of it, but she couldn't. It just wasn't her world.

He sighed. "I don't know."

Lisa shifted, turning toward him, desperate to figure out what made him tick. "You're really not making much sense."

Braden shifted toward her also, his gaze warm yet curious on her. "You really want to know?"

"I do."

"You might think I'm crazy."

Lisa smiled. "I already think you're crazy."

"At least you're honest." His chuckle quickly faded, and the heaviness returned around him. "I . . . uh, I keep blacking out. Anything traumatic in my life seems to trigger my brain to shut down. My therapist said it's normal after a brain injury like the one I suffered."

"So, for that reason, you can't remember who's trying to kill you?"

"It's pretty complicated, I suppose. But it's like my body is in fight-or-flight mode all the time. It senses that I'm in danger, but I can't remember any of the details."

"And that means you wouldn't recognize the person behind the threats."

He nodded. "That's right. I know it sounds insane. But . . . that's the gist of it."

Lisa pulled her knees to her chest, deep in thought. "Do you have any idea who it might be?"

"A couple ideas." Braden let out a long breath. "I helped stop a major terrorist attack in Washington, DC, sabotaging it before it ever even reached these shores."

Lisa sucked in a quick breath. "What? A terrorist attack? I never heard about one in Washington, DC."

"That's because we stopped it. The Revolt had planned it."

"The Revolt?" Lisa *had* heard of them. They'd been on the news often enough. They were a group of extremists who were only bonded by one thing: their hatred of America. They'd been responsible for hacking into the social media accounts of several key political leaders and exposing embarrassing information about them.

"Yes, they were hoping to take their attacks to the next level. They'd planned on hacking into DC's metro line and wreaking havoc. It would have been devastating."

"I had no idea."

"Believe me, if the American public knew what I knew . . . what people who are truly on the front lines of fighting terrorism know . . . they wouldn't sleep at night. It's better if people can just continue on in ignorant bliss because there's some scary stuff out there."

Lisa shivered beside him. "I bet."

"But, yeah, we heard about what this group was planning. When my colleagues got to the Metro to thwart the attack, they discovered The Revolt had gone a step further. They'd not only attacked the technology that operated the train, but they'd planted a bomb at the entrance to one of the stations."

"That's horrible."

"I was overseas in Latvia. My mission was to try to pinpoint The Revolt's base of operations there. I managed to find their hideout, and, with a little creativity, I convinced these guys to tell me how to disarm the bomb. I relayed the information back to my colleagues here in America."

"It sounds like you were some kind of liaison between the military and the CIA."

"You could say that. My job was commissioned by the president himself."

"No way."

"There were actually five of us on this team, but we usually operated independently."

"You were like Jason Bourne, weren't you?"

He let out a chuckle. "Not exactly. The assignments were off the books, though."

"But you're not denying it, either."

Lisa let that thought settle on her. Certainly that

would be reason enough for someone to want him dead. To want revenge and to make him pay.

She needed to be prudent and remind herself just whom she was getting involved with here.

Memories of the incident began to pummel him, and Braden shifted. He didn't often talk about this stuff, only with his therapist. But Lisa was so willing to listen. And she was . . . amazing.

"Did The Revolt know you were responsible for stopping their attack?" Lisa asked.

"Word leaked, and it's one of the reasons I got out of the military when I did. I knew I was putting everyone around me in danger by remaining. I was the number one target on The Revolt's hit list, and they weren't going to stop until they got their revenge."

She leaned lower to catch his eye. "So you think it might be one of these guys who's trying to kill you now?"

Braden shrugged. "Maybe."

Lisa shifted, her full attention on him, and she looked sincere—not disbelieving or like she wanted to run. "Why do you think they found you?"

"I've gotten a few texts that are suspicious, indicating someone is watching me."

She shivered again and something close to a flash of recognition lit in her eyes. "I'm sorry to hear that."

"Yeah, me too. My psychologist wonders if a lot of this is in my head. If it's the aftereffects of war and my body is programmed to be in this state of fight or flight."

"Is this therapist of yours worth his salt?"

"Dr. Larson? Yeah, he's good. Really good. I actually served with his son overseas after I first enlisted. Dr. Larson and his wife, Laura, became like a second family to me. And the doctor is one of the best in the business. He's grown an empire, to be honest, with his EMDR therapy."

"EMDR?"

"It's this revolutionary new therapy that helps people with PTSD. It's like cognitive therapy, only faster. Through talking about the event that caused your trauma, you can actually forget it. Well, not totally forget it. But forget enough."

"You said people wonder if this is all in your head." Lisa pulled her knees closer to her chest, looking cozy and inviting and comfortable. "What do you think?"

"I don't know what to think anymore, to be honest."

She rested her palm against the side of his face. "You're going to get through this."

Warmth spread through his chest, and he leaned closer. It felt good to have someone believe in him, to not look at him like he was crazy. "You really think so?"

"I do. Look what you've already overcome . . . you've got this, Braden."

Lisa's words did something to his heart. Gave him hope. To have someone believe in him . . . it was more healing than Braden would have ever guessed.

"You're a special woman, Lisa," he murmured.

She squeezed his hand, and the tremors disappeared again.

"Can you just keep holding my hand? It's the only thing that seems to help me."

"Of course. Just tell me how long."

"How about forever?" He cleared his throat, realizing what he'd just said. "Or I'll just take this week. Whatever I can get."

She grinned. "Sure thing."

His lips met hers again. He could do this every day. For the rest of his life.

The thought sent a wave of shock through him.

He'd never thought long-term like that before. No, he'd always been content by himself.

But Lisa was different. Even though Braden hadn't known Lisa that long, he knew a good thing when he saw it.

And Lisa was definitely a good thing.

But fear remained in the back of his mind, fear that his presence might end up getting Lisa hurt.

And he'd never forgive himself if that happened.

Chapter Fifteen

LISA LEANED INTO BRADEN, surprised at how comfortable she already felt around the man. It didn't seem normal.

And maybe that was what made it so great.

Some people might say that she'd lost her mind . . . but she actually felt like she'd just found it.

So many fireworks were exploding inside her that she felt like she might burst with joy. Who would have thought that the man of her dreams would enter her life like this? But now she never wanted it to end.

Braden pulled away and let out a deep sigh. "I should go."

She quirked an eyebrow at him, challenging his assumption. "Should you?"

He smiled and ran his finger down the side of her face before tapping her nose playfully. "I'd hate to tarnish your reputation by staying too late. I know how small towns work."

"Everyone who knows me knows my character," she said. "I'm not scared. But thanks for thinking of me."

They unwrapped themselves from each other and climbed down the ladder to Lisa's apartment and then down the stairs into the restaurant.

They paused by the front door, and Braden pulled her into his arms again.

He seemed to share her feelings—and the sentiment that neither could seem to get enough of the other.

It was so crazy. Lisa knew it was. But . . . Lisa had never felt like this before. Despite her hesitancies, her desire to take the plunge was greater, stronger.

Braden's lips met hers once more, and Lisa lingered in his embrace.

"So, how was it?" Braden murmured.

She kept her arms around his waist, amusement rushing through her. "How was what?"

"Your first kiss?"

Lisa raised an eyebrow. "You fishing for compliments?"

Braden chuckled, a deep, rich sound that she could listen to forever. It washed over her like a warm balm that soothed the ragged edges of her soul.

"I just don't want to disappoint you," Braden said.

"Oh, I'm not disappointed." Lisa was nearly overwhelmed, but she didn't want him to get a big head about it. In all the moments she'd imagined her first kiss, none of them had been this good. Not even close.

"Well, maybe we could try it again sometime, just to be sure." His voice held a teasing sound that delighted her.

"Okay, I think we can do that."

He smiled down at her, some kind of unseen force zapping around them, drawing them together and connecting them. "It was really fun tonight, Lisa."

"Yeah, it really was."

Something deeper glimmered in Braden's gaze as he paused, on the verge of saying something yet hesitating. "I know I don't have much game, that I'm supposed to hold my cards close."

"I hate playing games." She really did.

Life—and relationships—might require strategy at times, but never did it require toying with other people.

"Truth be told," Braden said. "I haven't felt this happy in a long time."

A grin spread across Lisa's face. His words made her exceedingly happy. "Neither have I."

"Would you mind if I stopped by sometime in the morning?"

"You better or I'll sic Ty on you when he gets back. Better yet, how about if I bring breakfast to you?"

"I'd like that." Braden grinned again, started to lean close, but backed up instead. "I should go."

Lisa hated for him to leave, but it was a good idea. They were both too caught up in this moment and . . . it was just better if they had some space. Besides, they had tomorrow. And the next day. And the next.

"Are you sure I can't drive you?" she asked, glancing beyond him at the dark, cold island road.

Braden drew in a shaky breath. "No, it would be better if I walked. Believe me. I need to cool off a little."

"Okay. Goodnight then. Maybe I'll see you tomorrow."

"Maybe?"

She grinned. "We can make it definitely, if you'd like."

"I'd like."

"Okay, I'll definitely see you tomorrow."

She could hardly wait.

Braden grinned as he walked along the edge of the deserted road. It didn't even matter that it was freezing cold outside. No, he felt happier in this moment than he had in a long, long time.

He'd never thought when he'd come here that he'd meet someone like Lisa. Never thought that someone could so easily capture his heart. Someone could see past his brokenness like she had.

And now his thoughts were consumed. He couldn't wait to see her again. To spend time with her. To listen to her unique take on life and to see her wrinkle her nose as she laughed at her own corny jokes or delighted in her kitchen experiments. She was as one of a kind as her recipes were.

Braden's phone buzzed in his pocket. As he

pulled it out, he held his breath, hoping it wasn't another threat from whoever had been sending them. Instead, he saw Ty's name on his screen.

He put the phone to his ear. "Hey, Ty. What's going on?"

"Cassidy and I just got back to my parents' house from my mom's birthday party. I thought I'd call and check in."

Braden considered telling him about Lisa. About him. About *them*.

But he didn't. He wasn't ready to share it with anyone. Because as wonderful as it had been, it was just one night. He knew relationships were built on more than a single experience.

But Braden had a good feeling about this one.

"Things are going okay," he finally answered. His voice sounded lighter than it had in months.

"I'm glad to hear that. I've been praying for you."

"Prayers go a long way, so I appreciate it. I have a feeling things are getting better."

"That's one of the reasons I want to open Hope House in Lantern Beach. There's something about the sea and the saltwater that gives people clarity. It worked for me, at least."

Braden wished that everything sounded as clear

as Ty hoped it was. He remembered that picture of Lisa someone unknown had sent him. No, everything wasn't as rosy as he'd like. That fact lingered in the back of Braden's mind. For that reason, he hadn't left Lisa until she'd locked the door behind him, and he knew she was okay.

Ty paused. "No more incidents, right?"

Braden told Ty about the house being ransacked.

"You have no idea who's behind this?" Ty asked.

"Only vague theories," Braden said. "But I told Mac, and he's looking into it. You're going to regret inviting me here, aren't you?"

"No, I didn't say that. I just wish you'd truly been able to get away from it all."

"Me too, man. Me too."

Braden walked down the lane to Ty's place, listening to the crickets and frogs singing in the brush around him. The sound was cut by the mighty sound of the waves crashing in the distance.

Maybe Lantern Beach wasn't that bad after all. Though he lived in a beach town, this place had a unique charm all of its own.

He ended his call with Ty, shoved his phone in

his pocket, and climbed the steps to Ty's place, whistling a little tune to himself.

As Braden stepped inside, he heard a footfall behind him. Before he could turn and defend himself, someone came at him from behind.

And everything went black.

Chapter Sixteen

LISA FELT herself glowing as she paused outside the door to Ty's house the next morning.

She'd been glowing since last night and mentally replaying her time with Braden. She nearly wanted to pinch herself to make sure she hadn't dreamed it all.

She knocked at the door and shifted the basket full of muffins she'd baked to her other hip. She'd made two different flavors: candy corn and pumpkin praline. One day, she would stop using her friends as lab rats . . . maybe.

A moment later, the door opened, and a smile spread across her face as Braden came into view. He looked stiff and standoffish. Had she woken him? Maybe she should have called first. But he was dressed in jeans and a long-sleeved blue shirt that softened his features. He'd at least been awake for long enough to shower and dress.

"Hey, there," she murmured.

Braden nodded. "Hey, there. You're the person Ty hired to help with food, right?"

Lisa's stomach lurched. Certainly, she just hadn't heard him correctly. "I'm—I'm who?"

He squeezed the skin between his eyes. "I'm sorry—I can't remember your name."

"Lisa." The words sounded dull to her own ears. What was going on here? Her mind swirled as facts collided in her.

"Lisa, that's right. Thanks for coming by. I wasn't sure if you would after last time."

"Last time?" Did he mean when they'd kissed? Something fierce and prickly squeezed her heart so hard that her chest ached.

"When I put you in that chokehold. I apologize for that."

"When you put me in the chokehold?" Lisa's pulse throbbed harder. What was going on? This conversation made no sense. Was it a joke?

"Yeah, the last couple of days have been a blur. I feel like I got run over last night." He dragged his hand over his face again.

"Run over, huh?" Braden didn't remember any of their time together yesterday, she realized. Nothing.

What had he said earlier?

That he forgot traumatic things?

Was being with Lisa really that traumatic? Maybe it was.

Her heart raced as she stood there. No, this morning wasn't going anything like Lisa had hoped it would. Should she remind Braden about the connection they shared?

No, she decided. That would be awkward. And hearing about what a great connection they had would be different than actually remembering the experience for himself. He had to remember. It was the only way.

Braden shifted, still standing there and looking at her like she was a stranger. "Can I help you?"

"Yeah, I . . . uh, I brought you some breakfast." She thrust the basket into his hands, hating how awkward this felt.

He took it from her and glanced inside. "Oh, that was nice of you. Thank you."

"Listen, could I use your restroom for a minute?" Lisa needed to compose herself and maybe splash some water in her face before she passed out.

"Of course."

She skirted by him, feeling his body heat as she passed. She smelled his aftershave. Remembered his touch.

Lisa had been hoping too much when she'd thought that maybe they could have something. She'd been a fool to think so. No, she was back in sidekick status. The overweight best friend. The one guys acted chummy with, only because they wanted to date her friends. They were never interested in Lisa, never saw her as anything but a buddy. A pal.

Story of her life.

Maybe it was better this way.

She went straight to the bathroom, started the water, and splashed it in her face.

What was she going to do?

She had no idea right now.

Braden snapped his head toward the sound in the hallway. Lisa stepped out of the bathroom, a tight smile on her face. It was almost like there was something she wasn't saying . . .

Had he missed something? Was she still tense from when he'd put her in a chokehold? He couldn't blame her.

"Thanks for letting me use the bathroom," she said, rubbing her hands on her jeans before throwing her thumb over her shoulder. "I'll be going now."

"Thanks for the muffins."

She swallowed so hard that Braden could see the muscles in her neck tighten. "Enjoy."

As soon as she was gone, something felt empty inside Braden . . . a little lonelier.

It was just his brain playing tricks on him. His head had been pounding all morning.

He grabbed a muffin and sagged against the counter. Had something happened last night?

He didn't know. All he remembered was waking up in bed this morning. He'd just assumed he'd slept so soundly that he'd blocked everything else out.

Yet, logically, he knew there were big chunks of time missing. He remembered meeting Lisa after he'd first arrived here. He remembered wandering the island roads. Staring at the ocean. He vaguely even remembered going to a restaurant.

But that was it. He had no other memories of Lisa.

Should he?

As he glanced at the muffin, his gaze skimmed his hands.

His bruised hands.

He stretched out his fingers and examined the wounds there.

What had happened last night to injure his hands like this?

That familiar sense of brokenness echoed in his gut.

His mind wanted to believe everything was okay. But his gut told him it wasn't. In fact, his gut told him that things were far from okay.

Chapter Seventeen

LISA BYPASSED GOING HOME. Instead, she went to Skye's place—a retro trailer her friend kept parked at an area campground. Lisa rapped on the door. To her relief, Skye answered a couple minutes later.

Lisa had halfway figured her friend would be at Austin's already since the two were officially attached at the hip.

"Lisa?" Skye squinted, as if confused, and pulled her olive-colored duster sweater around her. Her hair was pulled back into a sloppy bun. Her friend had obviously just woken up. She was one of those rare people who could still look gorgeous with messy hair, sleepy eyes, and dumpy clothes.

"Can we talk?"

"Yes, of course. Come in." Skye opened her door wider.

Lisa stepped into the trailer, and they took a seat at the little booth that served as a kitchen table during the day. The scent of lavender essential oil filled the colorful space, a space that had always reminded Lisa a bit of a gypsy abode.

Skye had decorated with teal and colorful tiles and handmade pillows.

The space was home and fit Skye perfectly.

"Can I get you some tea?" Skye asked.

Lisa shook her head. "No, I'm okay. Thanks."

Instead, she twisted her hands together as she remembered her earlier conversation with Braden. "I'm in trouble, Skye."

"What's wrong?"

"I think I'm falling in love with someone who might be out of his mind."

Skye shrugged, like she'd been expecting to be handed a four-course meal and had been given an apple instead. "Well, it would be a great story to tell. Braden, right? I saw it coming. He's handsome and maybe a little rough but nothing you can't handle."

"I kissed him."

"You kissed him?" Skye leaned across the booth with wide, surprised eyes.

Lisa nodded, wishing she could relish the memory. But it was too late. She and Braden's time together felt tarnished. "It was so incredibly sweet and tender . . ."

A flash of his lips meeting hers amidst apple pie and a messy kitchen filled her with warmth. But as today's events smacked into yesterday's moments like a runaway train, the gooey feelings turned ice cold.

"I'm so happy for you, Lisa."

Lisa needed to put the kibosh on her congratulations—and quickly. "He's forgotten all of it, Skye. He said his doctor told him his brain forgets unpleasant things. I stopped by this morning, just like I told Braden I would, and he had no clue what happened between us. No clue. Apparently, our kiss was traumatic."

Skye frowned. "Lisa, just because he doesn't remember doesn't mean the kiss was traumatic."

"Well, he seemed to enjoy it at the time, but . . . I just don't know, Skye. It's like I reached the top of this beautiful mountain that has glorious views— only to fall to a violent death."

Skye winced as if the description physically hurt her. "Are you going to tell him it happened?"

"I don't know that either. I'd prefer that Braden remember it rather than me trying to tell him it was awesome but possibly traumatic for him."

Skye frowned and shook her head skeptically. "I doubt it was traumatic for him."

"What am I getting myself into, Skye? He has a brain injury, which apparently can cause him to be delusional and violent. I should be running far away. This is my chance to do just that. He doesn't remember a thing so, as far as he's concerned, we never happened."

"Why aren't you running then?"

"Because . . . I don't think that's who he is. I realize I don't know him well. But my gut tells me that the kind but tough man who's helped me out here is the real Braden. Does that sound crazy?"

"No, it doesn't. But let's say Braden does remember—you'll still need to be careful. I mean, what's the prognosis? Will he be like this forever? Will it pass?"

"I don't know. I hope so. It's strange but . . . he seems better when he's with me. When he gets the tremors and I touch him, he calms down."

Skye's expression turned dramatically dreamy. "That sounds really beautiful, Lisa."

"Or maybe I'm just a romantic. A hopeless romantic who's watched too many happy ever afters on TV. Maybe love—and I'm not saying I love him. It's too soon—but maybe love really can't conquer all."

"Maybe not. But I have to think it can conquer most things. It's helped me to conquer demons in my past, and my past has had some pretty dark moments." Skye leaned closer. "So what are you going to do?"

"I have to figure that out." Lisa stared into the distance. "Pray for wisdom, okay? Because I don't want to mess up here. Not when the results could have lasting effects. Not just for me. But possibly for Braden."

Lisa wiped beneath her eyes. Where had the moisture come from? From disappointment, she realized. Painful, raw disappointment.

"Oh, Lisa."

"It's ridiculous. I've only known the man for three days. I shouldn't feel like this." She fanned her face, willing her tears to stop.

"Feel like what?"

"Heartbroken." Lisa's throat burned as she said the words. "Like I said, it's ridiculous. I know it is."

"It's not ridiculous if you guys had a connection —a strong, unique connection. Anyone would mourn the loss of something like that."

Just then, Lisa's phone rang. She glanced down and saw Mac's number on the screen. "Hey, what's going on?"

"Hey, Lisa. Listen, could you swing by the station for a minute? I went by the restaurant and you weren't there."

"Yeah, of course. Is everything okay?" Had he figured out who shot her window?

"I think so. I just have a few questions for you."

She sucked in a long, deep breath and tried to pull herself together. "I'll be right there."

It was a good thing she had nothing else to do today.

Lisa felt uneasy as she stepped into the chief's office at the police station. She spotted Mac riffling through some papers in the corner filing cabinet and lightly knocked on the door to let him know she was here.

Mac turned, but his smile slipped when he spotted her, replaced with hesitation of some sort. "Lisa. Thanks for coming. Have a seat."

After that reaction, the bad feeling in her gut grew.

There had to be more to this story. Mac could have told her the basic facts over the phone. But for some reason he'd wanted her to come in so they could talk face-to-face.

Mac shut the door before sitting behind his desk. He laced his hands together and paused, as if gathering his thoughts. "John Linksi was found beaten this morning."

Lisa's eyes widened, unsure if she'd heard correctly. "What?"

Mac nodded in confirmation. "He was found on the side of the road, not terribly far from your restaurant."

"I . . . I see. I'm sorry to hear that. How is he?"

"He's in critical condition and has been taken up to the hospital in Norfolk. His injuries were severe enough to warrant the transfer."

"Wow." Lisa didn't like the man, but she would have never wished this on him.

Mac smoothed the curling edge of the desk calendar beneath his elbows. "He hasn't woken up yet, so he can't tell us what happened. That's why I asked you to come in."

She shifted, suddenly uncomfortable. There was more to this story, but Lisa wasn't sure she wanted to hear it. "I don't understand . . ."

"Obviously we're looking into people who had bad feelings toward the man."

Lisa sucked in a quick breath at the implications of his statement. "You think I did it?"

Mac chuckled, breaking the tension in the room. "No, I don't think you did it. But you have had some confrontations with the man recently, haven't you?"

"Yes, but I would never do something like this."

"Calm down, calm down." He patted the air, his voice placating. "I didn't bring you in as a suspect."

"Then why did you bring me in?"

"Like I said, I want to ask some questions."

"I don't understand . . ." If she didn't do it, then what would she know? This didn't make sense.

Mac shifted in his seat, that heaviness returning to him. "Someone identified another man walking along the street last night around the same time John was beaten up."

Her shoulders relaxed ever so slightly—but

prematurely. The optimist in her wanted to emerge, yet she could sense bad news was coming. "That's great. You do have a suspect then. John, despite his faults, deserves justice."

Mac's gaze locked with hers, and everything around her seemed to disappear. "Lisa, what do you know about this man you've been spending time with lately?"

"The man I've been spending time with? You mean Braden?" Things tried to click in her mind, but she didn't want them to. No, an inkling of the bigger picture showed her something she didn't want to face.

"Yes, Braden. What do you know about him?"

The sour feeling in her stomach grew. "He was Special Forces. He has some memory problems and a brain injury because of a war injury. But he's . . . he's harmless."

"You don't think he could hurt someone?"

"Oh, he could hurt someone. But that doesn't mean he would." Lisa could feel the hole she was digging herself in. The problem was, she was already in too deep to pull herself out.

"You've never been threatened by him?"

The first night they met flashed back into her head. Had Lisa told Mac about that? It didn't matter. She couldn't lie. "Well, yes. But it was a misunderstanding—"

"What time did Braden leave your place last night, Lisa?"

She nibbled on her bottom lip for a moment, wishing she didn't have to answer. Instead, she begrudgingly said, "11:30."

"Have you talked to him today?"

"I have."

"How did he seem?"

There was no use trying to keep the information from Mac. Hiding it wouldn't be beneficial to anyone—even if her heart felt like it was breaking. "He . . . he had a memory lapse. He only remembers the first day we met but nothing after that."

Mac let out a subtle grunt. "Do you know what causes these memory lapses?"

"Trauma."

"Like a fight?"

Lisa licked her dry lips—lips that matched her throat and maybe even her heart. "Maybe."

"Did he know that John had been giving you a hard time?"

Their confrontation at the restaurant flashed back into Lisa's mind, and she nodded. "Yeah, he did."

Mac straightened. "Okay, that's everything I need to know. Thanks for your help."

"Are you going to bring Braden in?"

"I don't have much choice. I'm sorry, Lisa. I know it's not what you want to hear. But it's the right thing to do. And doing the right thing is my job."

Chapter Eighteen

BRADEN STARED at the police chief, certain he hadn't heard the man correctly. "You think I did what?"

Mac shifted in front of him as they stood just inside the front door at Ty's house. "We're investigating the beating of a man named John Linksi."

"Why would I beat this man up? I don't even recognize his name." Alarm coursed through Braden. With his memory issues, he had difficulty defending himself. Losing large chunks of time left him feeling helpless—and he hated feeling helpless.

Mac's eyes narrowed. "You don't remember him coming into the Crazy Chefette and threatening Lisa Garth?"

Braden's eyes widened at the man's words, at

the memory of the sweet, petite woman who'd left muffins. "Lisa Garth? The woman who stopped by this morning with breakfast?"

An unreadable expression came across Mac's face. "I believe that's correct. I can't verify the breakfast part of the equation. You really don't remember anything other than that about Ms. Garth?"

Braden shrugged. "No. Should I?"

"I can't answer that question either. But she did confirm that John Linksi came into her restaurant two nights ago, and you stepped in to protect her."

"Okay . . . what's the problem?" Braden knew there was something he was missing, and he hated it. He hated these gaps in his memory.

"Mr. Linksi was found nearly beaten to death on the side of the road last night. Another witness places you on the road around that same time."

Braden shook his head. No, not again. His body and mind were failing him. Acting out of his control. "I don't know what to say. I don't recall any of that."

"You have memory issues, is that correct?"

"I had a head injury that happened while I was doing a mission over in Iraq. A bomb exploded, and the force of it threw me back so fast and hard that my skull cracked. I've been through therapy, and now I'm on medication to help me."

"Do you remember last night?"

Braden wanted to lie. But he couldn't. Besides, lies always caught up with a person and were never a good idea. "Actually . . . I don't. Sometimes I black out."

"Mr. Dillinger, could I see your hands?"

His stomach sank as dread pooled inside him. "I didn't do this."

"Can I see your hands?" Mac repeated.

He closed his eyes knowing exactly how this was going to look. Finally, he jerked his arms up, displaying his scraped and bruised knuckles.

He didn't know how it happened. He woke up this morning, and they'd ached. Hurt.

He'd figured he'd had a bad dream and had punched the headboard.

Not that he'd beaten up someone.

Could he really have done this?

Based on the look in Mac's eyes, Braden could have . . . and it would be hard to prove to anyone otherwise.

"So, let me get this straight," Wes said. "You met this Braden Dillinger guy four days ago. You thought he was going to kill you, but then you ended up liking him. Really liking him. But now he's forgotten you, and he may have nearly beaten someone to death?"

Lisa squeezed the skin between her eyes. "Yes, I guess you could sum it up that way. I wouldn't have used those exact words."

She'd called an emergency meeting of her friends . . . mostly because she had no idea what else to do or how else to sort through her thoughts.

They'd all shown up here at the Crazy Chefette an hour later.

And that hour while waiting for them to arrive had nearly done her in. She hadn't been able to sit still with her thoughts. No, instead she'd decided to cook. Keeping Thanksgiving in mind, she made some fried mashed potato balls with goat cheese, pumpkin pecan bread pudding, apples stuffed with sausage and cornmeal, and a bacon and mayonnaise wrapped turkey breast.

Now the place smelled like Thanksgiving, and a feast had been set up on the table so her friends could eat while they listened to her problems. Food always made everything better.

If only that were true.

There was no way food could truly make this better. No, it would only make it more pleasant.

By training, Lisa was a scientist. She created hypotheses and tested them. Sometimes, those hypotheses were proven correct. Other times, she'd been proven dead wrong.

Had she been dead wrong when it came to Braden?

"Maybe you should stay away from him, Lisa," Austin said. He sat at the table, beside Skye—of course—and he grabbed his second mashed potato ball.

Apparently, they were a favorite out of everything she'd made because they were going fast.

She understood where Austin was coming from but . . . "I don't think he would have done this."

"You said the timeline fits, right?" Wes had come directly from kayaking, and he still wore a wetsuit, along with a knit hat on his shaved head. "That Braden left here at 11:30, and that John was beat up not long after? And that his body was found between your place and Ty's?"

Lisa nodded, the bad feeling in her gut growing worse by the moment. She knew how this looked and sounded. And, if she were in her friends' shoes, she'd tell herself to run as quickly as she could from this man.

The problem was, she didn't want to run. She'd been trying to convince herself to do just that all morning, and it hadn't worked. No, she was more determined than ever to stay and fight.

"But . . ." Lisa didn't even know what she was going to say. Finally, she hung her head and sighed. "I've got nothing."

"If not Braden, then who might have done it?" Wes asked.

"I don't know. I mean, someone shot out my window. And—" Lisa stopped herself.

"And what?" Austin tilted his head and leaned closer as he waited for her to finish.

"It's probably nothing," she said, wanting to take back what she'd started to say.

Wes crossed his arms and stared at Lisa. "Let us be the judge of that."

"The other night, someone was standing outside my place. I'm pretty sure he took a picture. I saw a flash."

"And you're just now mentioning this?" Wes's voice held surprise and maybe a touch of agitation.

"I figured it was my imagination going wild." Now that Lisa said it out loud, she realized that maybe she should have said something. There was nothing normal about that.

"Was Braden with you when you saw the figure and the flash?" Austin asked.

Lisa shook her head.

This was looking worse and worse. She couldn't even deny it. Every time something strange had happened, Braden was away.

Or was he?

Since Lisa couldn't offer him an alibi, did that mean he really might be the one responsible?

"Will you just listen to me for a minute, though." Lisa felt desperate to make her friends see things her way. "Someone is trying to kill Braden."

Her friends stared at her.

"I know it sounds crazy. But I saw the threat myself."

"What does this have to do with John?" Wes asked.

"What if . . . I don't know." Lisa searched for an explanation. "What if someone set Braden up?"

"I'm not saying I buy that explanation, but keep going," Austin said. "Who's trying to kill him?"

"He doesn't know. But he stopped a terrorist attack with a group called The Revolt. Apparently, he made a lot of enemies, and now they want to exact revenge on him."

"He was a part of that?" Skye's eyes widened, as if impressed. "The Revolt has some scary guys. I heard about them on the news, and I hardly ever watch the news."

"Yeah, they are scary. Deadly. And if they were to find out Braden's name, they'd do everything within their power to make him pay."

Wes shifted. "That sounds heroic and everything. If that's all true, then I'm impressed. Taking on people like that . . . it takes courage. But what if that really didn't happen? What if Braden is suffering from grandiose delusions or something?"

Everyone turned to stare at Wes.

Wes shrugged. "What? I like to read and keep up with current events. And I know some mental disorders involve delusions of grandeur."

"In some cases, I might believe you," Lisa said. "But Ty can verify his military service."

"True." Wes shrugged again.

Austin finished his food and leaned back, his eyes heavy with thought. "And you think one of these terrorists could have followed him here?"

"I'm just asking that we might explore that idea." Lisa glanced around the table. "Have any of you seen anyone strange in town? Wes, you see people when they come in for kayak tours. Skye, people stop by your produce stand to buy pumpkins and mums this time of year. Austin, you're a social guy. Anything?"

Her friends exchanged another look. "It would be hard to pinpoint members of The Revolt, Lisa. These guys look like European Americans. They blend in."

"I'm just asking about visitors. They are few and far between here on the island this time of year."

"There were two guys who stopped by the produce stand yesterday," Skye said. "They seemed like the hunting and fishing type. They were kind of quiet. I mean, I'm not saying they're killers . . ."

Lisa's pulse jumped. "Did they say anything?"

"Just that they're staying at one of the small cottages and that they come every year."

Lisa frowned. "Every year?" Someone who was a regular vacationer here was unlikely to be the person responsible.

"That's what they said."

Lisa glanced at Austin and Wes. "What about you two?"

Austin shrugged, looking a bit bewildered. "I've been wrapped up in some renovation projects. I haven't really seen anyone, other than the homeowners."

"It's true," Skye said. "He's been really busy."

Lisa looked at just Wes now. He was the last man standing.

He let out a long breath and shook his head. His features looked stony. And when Wes, someone who feared nothing and lived on adrenaline, looked nervous, it was never a good sign. "Listen, I really don't know. And I don't want to point the finger at anyone. I will say that I've seen a guy in town who seems out of place. He seemed urban, if you know what I mean. Not like the laid-back out-of-towners who go to the beach."

Lisa sat up straight. At least it was something. "Did you talk to this guy?"

Wes shrugged. "Not really. I worked on the plumbing at his rental."

"Think, Wes. Was there anything he said or did that might indicate he had less than honorable intentions for being here?"

Wes rubbed his jaw. "I think he said he was from Virginia Beach."

Her pulse spiked again. "Anything else?"

"Don't read too much into this." He raised a

hand, as if trying to slow down her thoughts. "But I do think he said he was here looking for someone."

Maybe that was the guy. Lisa had no idea the details or intricacies of her theories. She only knew she wanted to believe, more than anything, that Braden wasn't the guy responsible for this crime against John.

She wanted his memory to come back. Wanted for things to flip back and be like they'd been yesterday when she'd felt on top of the world. Why couldn't good things last forever?

Suddenly, something banged in the distance.

Lisa nearly jumped out of her seat.

She turned and saw Braden standing at the front door.

Did he finally remember her?

Or was he here because he was angry—angry because Lisa had given him up?

She had no idea. And she wasn't sure she wanted to find out.

Chapter Nineteen

BRADEN SAW Lisa sauntering toward the door, and his stomach clenched tighter. What was he doing here at the Crazy Chefette? What was he thinking showing up without an invitation?

He wasn't sure. Braden only knew that he was alone here on this island, with no one to believe him, no one to talk to, and a serious accusation thrown out against him.

Sometimes he'd welcome the isolation. But right now, he wanted answers. He wanted to know what had happened last night. And Mac had indicated Lisa might know.

As he stared at her kind, sweet face, his heart twisted. Why did he feel like he knew Lisa better than he did? Was there something he'd forgotten? By all indications, yes.

It just didn't make sense.

He remembered Mac. He remembered this restaurant. He vaguely remembered apple pie even.

So why had he forgotten Lisa?

She cracked the door open just a smidgen, hesitation evident on her features. "Yes?"

As a brisk wind brushed across his exposed skin, he rubbed his hands together. "I'm sorry to show up here like this, but I was hoping to ask you some questions."

She glanced behind her, and Braden saw people at a table there.

Her friends.

He recognized them—though he didn't remember their names. But they'd all met. Why did he remember that but not Lisa?

Lisa stared at him another moment before opening the door and letting him step inside.

He tried to read her expression. She was hesitant, definitely. Maybe a little nervous. But was there more to it? She almost seemed sad also. But why? What was he missing?

As soon as the door closed, one of her friends appeared beside her. A man with a close shaved head and a lean, sculpted build. Maybe his name was Wes. Why did Braden remember that but not Lisa?

"What's going on?" the man asked, obviously protective of Lisa.

"Please, I just want to talk." Braden glanced at Lisa. "I'm trying to fill in some missing memories, and I was hoping you could help."

Lisa crossed her arms, not in defiance. No, it was more of a protective measure. Was she scared of him? If so, why? "What do you need to know?"

Braden shoved his hands into his pockets. "I need to know what happened last night."

Her cheeks reddened ever so slightly, and she rubbed her lips together. She and Wes glanced at each other, some kind of silent conversation taking place.

Finally, she nodded, as if accepting Braden's presence here. "Okay. Why don't you have a seat? I'm going to need some coffee for this. You?"

"I'd love some." Braden ran a hand over his face, feeling exhausted from today's turn of events. It was strange how, only hours earlier, he'd felt invigorated and refreshed.

Now all of that had changed.

He balled his hands into tight fists before

releasing them and stretching his aching fingers. Then he did it again.

"Lisa, Skye and I have to leave," the other man said. "The guy is coming to check the septic system at that house we're flipping, and he should be there in ten minutes. Will you be okay?"

"I'm going to stay with her," Wes said, his voice hard.

"We'll be fine." Lisa held up a cup of coffee as if it were the magical solution that made everything better.

Wes didn't look as sure, but Braden couldn't blame him for wanting to stay. There were too many missing pieces for anyone to let their guard down.

Lisa handed Braden his drink and nodded toward a booth. "Let's sit."

Braden felt more nervous than he thought he would as he slid in across from Lisa and Wes. Neither of them said anything. They just waited for him to start.

The problem was, he hardly knew where to begin.

"The only thing I remember from yesterday was walking here," Braden said, blurry images filling his mind. "And I remember fixing a window. But everything else is a blur."

Lisa blinked and swallowed hard. "You don't remember anything else?"

He shrugged and took a sip of coffee. "I remember meeting you, Wes. But the first time I remember you, Lisa, is from the very first day I came into town. And then there's nothing else until this morning."

"Where did that other time go?" Wes said.

"I have memory issues. Big blocks of time are often black for me. But never that big of a time period." Braden shook his head as another memory tried to surface. "It's weird. I feel like there's a vague recollection trying to surface. It has to do with apple pie."

Lisa's eyes lit. "We ate apple pie yesterday. I experimented with recipes, and you were my guinea pig."

Braden was her guinea pig? He'd assumed the two of them had practically been strangers. Was there more to their background? He felt like he was lost with no roadmap to follow and failing instincts.

"I can't remember the man I supposedly beat up either." He absently rubbed the side of his coffee mug.

"John came in here and gave me a hard time," Lisa said. "You stepped in and . . . and protected me . . . until he went away."

"And I was here last night? Until 11:30?" His head pounded as he tried to make sense of things.

"That's right. You left and insisted you wanted to walk home." She took a long sip of her coffee.

"And, according to the police, I may have run into this John guy as I walked?"

"If you did, it would have to be because he was waiting for you," Lisa said. "To my knowledge, you had no idea where he lived."

"That's the impression I got from Mac also. The only reason I would have run into that man was if he'd planned it. I couldn't have hunted him down." If the man had confronted him, would Braden have done this to him? Only if he'd been defending himself.

"It did, at one point last night, sound like someone rattled the front doors, as if trying to get in." Lisa dragged her gaze up to him.

"Maybe John?" Braden questioned.

Lisa shrugged. "Maybe."

"What if I did this?" The thought wouldn't leave his mind.

Lisa leaned closer, no hints of judgment in her

eyes, only compassion. "Braden, you told me that someone was trying to kill you. Do you remember that?"

His spine clenched tighter at the reminder. He'd trusted her enough to tell her that? It wasn't something he just told anyone. "Yeah, I can't forget that."

"What if someone set you up?"

Lisa's words startled Braden. "Why would they do that?"

"Because they said they were coming for you."

His mind raced through the texts he'd discovered.

"Maybe we could find the person who is responsible."

"Lisa . . ." Wes said. His voice held caution. He didn't approve of her idea.

And he probably shouldn't.

"I'm just brainstorming—doing what I do best and putting out a hypothesis that we may want to test."

"I appreciate that, but testing new recipes is a lot less risky than testing out theories that could put your life at risk." Wes turned to Braden. "Listen, do all of these blackouts occur at night?"

"Usually. Why?"

"If you are innocent—and I don't know you well enough to know if you are or not—then something is happening at night. Have you ever set up a video camera?"

"Funny you ask that. I did try it once, but in the morning it had been knocked over, and there was nothing on it."

Wes exchanged another glance with Lisa.

"Maybe Austin and I need to stay over there with you tonight. We need to get to the bottom of what's going on. The only way we're going to do that is by finding out what happens when you black out."

"I'd do anything to find answers." Braden just hoped those answers were what he wanted to hear and didn't incriminate him further.

Wes nodded slowly. "Okay then. Let me talk to my friends, and we can plan on doing that. Listen, you're a friend of Ty's, and that means you're a friend of ours. I want to help you. I really do. I just don't want anyone getting hurt in the process."

By *anyone*, he had a feeling Wes meant Lisa.

Braden didn't remember much about Lisa, but he knew that he didn't want her getting hurt either.

Chapter Twenty

LISA GLANCED at Wes as he sat on guard beside her. Her throat burned as pressure seemed to mount around her.

She desperately wanted to talk to Braden. Alone.

Clearing her throat, she turned toward her friend, praying her words would be well received. "Wes, you can go. I know you have things to do today."

His eyes narrowed, as if he was trying to read her. "I don't mind staying."

Lisa touched his arm, trying to reassure him. "Really. I'll be okay."

It didn't work. Wes was too good a friend to simply leave, especially if Lisa might be in danger.

He was in protective mode, and he wasn't going to back down this easily.

"Can I talk to you a minute? Outside?"

"Of course." Lisa knew exactly what was coming, but she followed Wes outside anyway.

The bright sun showered them in a lemonade-colored light. But, despite the sunny day, the wind was still cold. It might be forty degrees outside, but the breeze easily made it feel below freezing.

She looked up at Wes and the determined, assessing look in his eyes. One day, he'd be a great boyfriend. He wasn't Lisa's type—and he wasn't ready to settle down—but he was strong and smart. He was cultured and informed, yet up for an adventure.

And all of his smart, informed attention was on Lisa now. "Are you sure you're safe alone with this guy?"

She nodded. "Yeah, I'm sure."

He glanced at Braden inside at the table. "He could have beaten that guy to a pulp. You don't know what he's capable of."

"I'm not scared of him, Wes. I know how that might sound—like I'm naïve or too optimistic for my own good. But I'm trusting my gut here, and my gut is telling me that he's okay."

Wes still didn't look convinced as he shifted his weight. "Look, you're a grown woman, Lisa, and you're capable of making your own choices. I just don't want anything to happen to you."

"He won't hurt me, Wes."

He continued to study her, a good dose of skepticism in his gaze. "You really like this guy, don't you?"

Lisa's throat burned as she contemplated what to say. *Why deny it?* she finally decided.

She shoved a hair behind her ear. "Yeah, I do."

"I hope this all works out then. You can call me if you need me. I'll come right away."

"I know. And I really appreciate that—more than you can know." She truly was grateful for her friends. They were lifesavers, in more ways than one.

Wes cast one more glance back inside before heading toward his truck.

Lisa felt the jitters racing through her as she stepped back inside the restaurant. She'd talked tough, but now she had to face Braden. She prayed she'd made a wise choice.

"Your friend left," Braden said, glancing behind her.

"He did."

Braden's eyes were soulful as he looked up at her. And maybe that's what got to her. It was like she could glimpse into his soul, and she saw the gentleness beneath the tough exterior.

She slid into the booth across from him, her muscles feeling wired and the neurons in her brain firing so rapidly she could hardly keep up. "Now we need to prove that you didn't beat up John."

His eyebrows shot up. "How are we going to do that?"

"I have one lead I'd like to follow." It was a long shot. Lisa knew it was. But she needed something.

Curiosity sparked in Braden's gaze. "What's that?"

"We're going to have to drive there. I can tell you in the car."

He still didn't move. "I don't want to pull you into the middle of anything unsafe."

"You're not. This is my idea. Besides, you'll be there to protect me."

His gaze locked with hers, no hint of teasing in the depths of his eyes. "What if I'm the one you need protection from?"

"You're not." Lisa heard the certainty in her voice. It was there because it was true. She really didn't believe Braden would hurt her.

"You seem convinced."

She offered an affirmative nod. "I am."

Braden stood, pulling himself to full height— full imposing height. "Okay then. Let's go. Because there's nothing more that I want right now than a good lead."

As Braden sat in Lisa's small sedan, the scent of watermelon and patchouli teased his senses.

He closed his eyes.

Why did that combination seem so familiar?

Memories felt like they wanted to fight their way through the fog—yet they couldn't. The harder Braden tried to claw through the mist, the more closed off the recollections became.

And Braden was left with only an inkling, some type of vague emotion in place of actual facts.

He glanced over at Lisa as she sat behind the steering wheel. Saw her delicate features. Her sparkling eyes. The determined set of her jaw.

Normally, she wouldn't be his type. At least, she wouldn't be the type of woman the old Braden would like. The old Braden liked to go to clubs and meet women who were out just looking for a good time.

No, Lisa was the kind of woman a guy met and wanted to marry.

Back in Braden's wilder days, he would have run far from that type because marriage was the last thing on his mind.

But maybe some good had come from his injury. It had brought him back to God. Brought him back to what was important in life.

He'd put those wild days behind him.

Lisa turned the car around at the end of a lane. A massive sand dune now stood protectively behind them, and a row of houses were before them. Most of the homes looked empty, probably the result of tourist season being over with. But one house—a smaller one with aged cedar siding—had a Volvo sedan in the driveway.

He could only assume that was the house they were keeping an eye on.

"So, you want to tell me what we're doing here?" he finally asked.

Lisa shoved on some aviator sunglasses and nodded toward the aforementioned house. "You told me that someone from The Revolt is trying to kill you."

"Wow. I usually don't talk about that." Had he lost his mind? That information . . . it was what he shared with his therapist. Maybe his comrades in arms. Maybe the police.

But not strangers.

Then again, Lisa hadn't been a stranger to him, had she? Somewhere in the back of his mind, he knew that.

Lisa shrugged, sadness grazing her features. "Maybe my apple pie warmed you up."

Apple pie . . . there was more to that memory, wasn't there? He'd ask more about that later. Right now, what he really wanted to know why they were here and what Lisa hoped to prove.

"So who do you think is in that house?" He stared at the cottage in the distance.

"I have it on good authority that the man staying here is from Virginia Beach, and he's here looking for someone."

"There are probably a lot of people in this area who come down from Virginia Beach, don't you think?" Braden had been hoping for something a little more solid.

"Yes, there are."

"And is looking for someone that unusual?"

She let out a soft breath, the first sign of exhaustion and doubt creeping in. "I don't know, to be honest. Doing stuff like this? It's not my thing. But there are so few visitors on the island this time of year. If someone did follow you here . . . the options are limited. It shouldn't be terribly hard to pinpoint who this person is."

"I see."

"I'm not saying we need to take action or anything. I'm just saying that maybe you'll see this person and recognize him. Maybe you'll be able to get some answers. It's . . . well, it's all I've got."

Braden turned toward Lisa, studying her face for a moment and trying to find answers that weren't within his grasp. "Why do you want to help me so much, Lisa?"

Her cheeks reddened again.

It was adorable how they did that when she felt embarrassed—not that Braden wanted to embarrass her. But the reaction was so genuine and refreshing.

She shrugged. "I just . . . I just think everyone needs someone."

There was more to that explanation. Braden could hear it in her voice.

Desire burned inside him. Desire for answers. For normalcy. For . . . resolution.

"What happened to your hands?" she asked, her voice cracking.

He glanced at his knuckles. "I have no idea."

"I'm sorry to hear that." Her voice contained a certain wistfulness that had him curious.

"Lisa, what am I forgetting? I feel like it's something important and—"

Before he could finish his question, Lisa's arm jutted out. "There he is! Do you recognize him?"

Braden swiveled his head toward the house just as a man emerged. He appeared to be in his forties, with a black leather jacket, stylish sunglasses, and polished shoes.

All in all, it wasn't the look most people here on the beach employed.

The man flipped some keys in his hands before climbing into his sedan.

Braden held his breath, waiting for a sign of recognition. But, first, he needed a better glimpse of the man's face. Because, right now, he had nothing.

Chapter Twenty-One

LISA'S GAZE veered back and forth between the man emerging from the house and Braden. Braden's expression didn't show anything, though. No recognition. Nothing.

Lisa had waded out into hope, she realized. Unreasonable hope. And she'd waded too deep, until it was no longer safe.

What if this whole situation didn't have the happy ending she was searching for? What if, instead, it left her feeling more in over her head than before?

No, she couldn't think like that.

This could be it. This man could be the explanation they were looking for.

"Anything?" Lisa's voice cracked as the word left her throat.

Braden shook his head—quickly. Too quickly to be relaxed or casual, yet quickly enough to show his frustration.

He ran his hand over his face. "I don't know. But I don't think so."

Lisa's gaze swerved back to the man. "He's going somewhere."

"What are you suggesting?"

"That we follow him." Lisa cranked the car before Braden could argue.

"I'm not sure that's a good idea—"

She eased her car out behind the mystery man and followed him through town. Maybe it *wasn't* a good idea. But, again, it was all she had.

The man parked near the boardwalk—an area that stretched for a half-mile and was filled with shops, restaurants, and even a small carnival area.

Lisa pulled into a space at the edge of the same lot and opened her door, not wasting any time. "We should follow him."

Braden stepped out behind her. "What's this going to prove?"

"That's what we need to find out. Are you in?"

Braden nodded, glancing at the man who also

climbed out. "Yeah, yeah. I'm in. I just don't want to put you in a situation—"

"You're not putting me in anything, so no worries. Now, let's follow his guy before he gets away." The last thing she needed was to lose him.

"Okay, okay." He raised his hands in surrender.

Lisa watched as the man pulled something from his trunk. A duffel bag.

A duffel bag?

Why in the world was he bringing a duffel bag to the beach? Another red flag went up.

Lisa and Braden hurried toward the boardwalk and got there just as the man slipped into a store. They paused outside the big windows at the front of the place.

It was All for Fun and Fun for All—the town's toy store.

An interesting place for a grown man to go into by himself.

Lisa casually stood near the entrance, trying to ignore the cool breeze that swept across the ocean and chilled everything within reach. Turning carefully, she attempted to see beyond the window. A giant teddy bear blocked her view.

Of course.

She glanced over at Braden, who stood on the

other side of the door. His hands were stuffed in his pockets, making him look casual—or like he'd done this surveillance thing a million times before. Maybe he had. There was still so much she didn't know about him.

"You're still not sure if he looks familiar?" she asked Braden.

"Not really." He shrugged and glanced through the window again. "I mean, that's the thing with this terrorist group. I haven't seen all their faces. They could send an operative to kill me, and it might be someone I've never seen before."

She bit her lip, halfway disappointed. She had to figure out who'd beaten up John.

It was the only way to prove Braden was innocent . . . and that the two of them might have a chance.

Yet so much was working against them.

Namely the fact that Braden couldn't even remember the incredibly romantic moment they'd shared last night.

Lisa's heart sagged with disappointment at the thought.

Was she willing to live like this for the foreseeable future—knowing Braden could forget again? She didn't know. She only knew she saw something special in Braden, and she wasn't willing to let that go yet.

Nor was she willing to remind him of what they'd shared. No, Braden needed to remember that for himself.

Most of all, Lisa needed to remind herself to stay in check. At the end of all this, she might not get the results she wanted. Braden might not remember. Braden might not be innocent, for that matter. Lisa would be wise to keep those warnings fresh.

A moment later, the man emerged from the toy store. He didn't even give the two of them a second glance as he hurried out with a shopping bag in one hand and that duffel bag in the other.

Lisa and Braden glanced at each other before falling into step behind him. Normally the board-walk was bustling with people, but not today. No, today, it was only the three of them.

Which would make it harder for them to stay concealed.

The man glanced at his watch and quickened his steps even more. As he stepped around the corner of a building, Lisa heard a yell.

She sucked in a breath, wondering what was going on.

As she rounded the building, the man came into view again. A little boy—probably three years old—had his arms around the man. A woman, about the same age as the man, stood off in the distance, watching everything unfold.

The man was visiting his son, if Lisa had to guess. Maybe a visitation after a divorce? Lisa had no idea.

As if to confirm her thought, the boy yelled, "Daddy, I've missed you so much!"

Lisa knew one thing: this wasn't their guy.

As if to confirm it, the man unzipped his duffel bag and revealed a stuffed dog. The boy squealed and hugged the well-worn animal.

She released the air from her lungs and tried to hold back her disappointment. But she honestly had no idea where else to look for answers.

She wished she thought more like Cassidy. The police chief had a knack for finding answers. But Lisa wasn't programmed to think like an investigator. But she could, however, think like a scientist.

She glanced at Braden and saw a moment of disappointment wash over him also.

What was she going to do now?

She had no idea.

"I appreciate that you tried," Braden said, seeing the disappointment on Lisa's face as they both stood there on the bitingly cold boardwalk. They turned their back on the reunion scene. The false lead.

Lisa had really hoped this would work out. Her effort had been valiant, even if her theory had been incorrect.

"It was my best lead." She lowered herself—more like dropped—onto a nearby park bench.

"And I appreciate that. Maybe I just need to face the fact that when I black out, something very dark happens to me." He didn't want to believe it, but the facts were staring him in the face. The sooner he owned up to his deadly potential, the better it would be for everyone.

Lisa's gaze was filled with conviction as she glanced up at him. "I don't believe that."

Her belief in him was inspiring, but perhaps misplaced. He lowered himself beside her. "Why don't you believe that?"

"Because . . . I just can't see that side of you." She stared off in the distance and rubbed her hands against her jeans, almost like her palms were sweaty.

Yet it seemed too cold for that—unless she was dealing with some kind of internal heat.

Maybe he needed to help her see that side of him. He wasn't as innocent as Lisa might think. "I did some horrible things in the name of justice while I was in the military, Lisa."

"That doesn't mean you're doing them now."

Braden's heart hammered in his chest. He wanted to say more. To spell things out in detail.

Yet he didn't.

That part of his past was something he wanted to put to rest. He didn't find any joy in talking about or rehashing those moments.

And, if he did tell Lisa about some of the missions he'd been on, then certainly that bright-eyed look she was giving him now would be erased. He'd been on the verge earlier, but he just couldn't do it.

Something about her look brought him hope.

Someone believed him.

And that one person could make all the difference.

The burden of his past, his present, and his future pressed on him. He couldn't do this anymore. It was time to surrender to the truth.

"Listen, would you mind dropping me at Ty's

place?" he asked. "I think I need to talk to my therapist and then rest some. My head is beginning to pound."

"Of course." Was that more disappointment in Lisa's voice?

He didn't know. Maybe he was reading more into this than he should. Or maybe he was reading into it what he wanted to read into it. Either way, it shouldn't matter. The facts were the facts.

Braden would stay here for another week or so. Then he'd go back to his regular life.

Except he didn't like his regular life all that much. Living in recovery mode didn't feel much like living at all.

Still, the only alternative was staying here in Lantern Beach. But he had no place here, and as soon as Ty and his wife returned, Braden would need to leave before he tarnished their reputations as well.

Of course, he didn't want that.

No, what he needed was hope.

Hope like what he saw in Lisa's eyes.

"Let's go," Lisa stood and nodded toward the parking lot where her car was.

"You know, I just changed my mind," Braden said, finally acknowledging the pool of dread he felt at the thought of being alone. "Could you drop me off at the church instead?"

"The church?"

He nodded. "Yeah, as much as I need to talk to my therapist, maybe I need to talk to a pastor more."

"Okay then. I'll drop you off at the church. Jack's a good one to talk to."

"And I appreciate your friends offering to stay with me this evening. Maybe we'll finally get some answers." Or maybe Braden would finally be forced to face the truth.

"I hope we will get some answers."

Lisa had said "we." She was in this with him, wasn't she?

Braden wasn't sure if he felt delight or dismay at the thought.

Chapter Twenty-Two

LISA TRIED to push her troubled thoughts aside as she stepped into her empty, quiet restaurant. In the summer, the place was brimming with vivacity. Right now, it felt like a coffin—absent of life.

She paused by the back entry, by the door where Braden had fixed the window pane. In front of her, she could see the bullet mark on the wall.

So much had happened this week. Too much, maybe.

Yet, in another way, she felt as if she'd never be the same.

The last thing she wanted was to stay by herself with only her thoughts to contend with. Even the idea of experimenting with some new recipes didn't appeal to her at the moment. No, right now, she wanted answers. She wanted to put her questions to rest.

But she couldn't.

She had nowhere else to look for answers. And, as hard as she tried to come up with a new idea or theory, she couldn't. Life wasn't a lab where she could test the variables until something worked. No, she was out of variables.

Or was she?

As she wandered into the restaurant kitchen, she pulled out her phone and made a call. Cassidy answered on the second ring.

"Lisa! How are you?" Her friend's warm voice filled Lisa with instant comfort. "You coming up with any new recipes I'm going to have to try?"

"I've been working on a few things that you can try out at Thanksgiving." Lisa smiled as she thought about the feast she was planning for her friends. It would have her signature recipes all over it.

"I can't wait."

She paused by her sink, looking at all the pots and pans she'd dirtied this morning in her quest to make food and keep her mind occupied. If she kept doing that, she was going to gain all forty pounds back. "I'm sorry to interrupt you while you're away."

"Oh, there's no interrupting right now. Ty and his father went hunting. His mom is sleeping. And I'm just sitting here reading a book."

"I need your advice." Lisa turned on the water and added some soap to the sink. At least she could begin cleaning as she talked.

"I've got advice by the barrelful. You didn't say if it was supposed to be good advice or not, though." Cassidy was smiling—Lisa could hear it in her voice. "What's going on, my mad scientist friend?"

"It's about this guy staying at your place," Lisa started, still watching the water rise.

"Braden? Yeah, what about him? I don't know the man, but Ty has told me some stuff, including about that first night you met him. I'm so sorry."

"Yeah, I've gotten to know him since then, and he seems like a pretty good guy—despite our rough start."

"After you got past the initial chokehold he put on you? If Ty didn't vouch for this guy's character, I would think the guy was a total hotheaded jerk."

"I get that. The thing is, John Linksi was beat

up last night." Lisa felt her lips tugging down in a frown as she said the words.

"John—the town drunk?" Cassidy's voice lilted with surprise.

"He's the one." Lisa filled her in on the rest of the story.

"So, what you're saying is that everyone thinks Braden did it?"

"By all appearances, he does seem guilty. His hands . . . they're bruised."

"Oh." Cassidy's voice dropped. "That could definitely implicate him in the crime."

Lisa turned the water off, but instead of beginning to wash the dishes, she leaned against the oversized sink in contemplation instead. "I know. But I really don't think he did this, Cassidy. That's where I'm stuck. If he didn't do it, who did? I don't even know how to find answers."

"I'm sure Mac is looking into it. I wouldn't concern yourself over it. Especially if someone violent is involved. You don't want to put yourself in a bad situation."

"I know. And I don't. And I won't. I just need . . . and I don't know what I need." She let out a sigh. "I need hope, I suppose."

Cassidy didn't say anything for a moment. "So you don't think Braden did this. But in order to prove that he didn't do it, you need to prove that someone else did?"

"Right. I don't even know how to do that. If you were here, you would know just what to do. You're a natural at things like this."

"Oh, girl . . . I don't know." Cassidy's voice dipped. "I don't want to lead you into trouble. Do I need to remind you how many times I almost got killed in the past year alone?"

"No, I remember a lot of them. And I don't want to put myself in that situation either. I just don't know what to do." Cassidy had always found herself in the middle of trouble, it seemed. After the stellar way she handled things, it only made sense that she became police chief.

"Maybe John will wake up and remember something. Or Mac will find some DNA evidence that's been left behind. Maybe a footprint or a hair. And I'm sure he's looking for witnesses. Just try to trust the process, Lisa. I know it's hard."

"It is." It was tearing her apart inside.

"I'll be praying for you."

"I appreciate that, Cassidy. Thank you."

Just as Lisa ended the call, she heard a knock on her back door. What was up with all of her unexpected visitors lately? She didn't know.

She rushed through the kitchen, toward the space at the back, and saw a man through the window.

He had gray hair, glasses, and wore a suit.

Lisa had never seen the man before—but he looked unassuming enough.

Leaving the chain lock on the door, she cracked it open. Until she knew what was going on, she had to be cautious—most of the time, at least. "Can I help you?"

"I'm looking for Lisa Garth."

"I'm Lisa."

"Lisa, I'm Rick Larson. I'm Braden Dillinger's therapist. We need to talk."

———

Braden stepped inside the small, traditional sanctuary and paused. Jack Wilson stood on the platform, bending over to pick up something from the floor in the choir loft area.

Jack straightened when Braden walked in. As

recognition lit his eyes, he smiled. "Well, hello there. Braden, right? Come on in."

Braden stepped closer, apprehension pulling at him. "I hope I'm not interrupting."

"I'm picking up some lyric sheets. I wish our choir members were as loose with their vocal chords as they are with their trash." Jack smiled and hopped off the stage to meet him. "What brings you by?"

"Could we talk for a minute?"

"Of course. Why don't you come into my office?" He nodded at a door off the side.

"Actually, if you don't mind, could we sit out here?" Something about being in a cramped office made Braden feel suffocated. This sanctuary, on the other hand, with its tall ceilings, stained glass, and padded pews . . . it brought back memories of better times.

He'd grown up going to church with his grandparents, but he'd fallen away once he hit high school. It wasn't until after his head injury that he'd started coming back. But those early memories were full of warmth and love.

"Of course, we can stay out here," Jack said. "Pick your pew, and we'll make it work."

Braden already liked Jack. He liked his attitude. His confidence. His dedication to the church.

Braden sat on the front pew, his body molding into the well-used, wine-colored cushion. Jack sat a comfortable distance from him.

"What's going on?" Jack stretched his arm across the back of the pew, looking totally at home and at ease in the space.

Drawing in a deep breath, Braden launched into what he had to say. He told Jack everything that had happened since he arrived in town—the copper wires, the memory loss, feeling utterly helpless.

It felt good to have everything off his chest, but now he waited to see how Jack would react. Would he treat Braden like a guilty man? Would he become fearful as he realized what Braden was capable of? Or would he simply offer advice?

Jack's expression lost his happy-go-lucky candor, and the grimness of the situation lined his eyes. "I can see where you're facing a dilemma. A big one, at that."

"You can say that again."

Jack studied Braden a moment, his eyes wise and accessing. "You don't think you did this?"

"I don't think so. But I wish I knew. It's hard

since parts of my past are just . . . well, empty. Erased almost."

"I can only imagine." Jack nodded toward Braden's hands. "And you have no idea how that happened?"

"No idea. I woke up and my hands were sore. My clothes were fine. Nothing else was wrong. I assumed I had a bad dream and maybe punched something. And, no, there were no signs of that. I'm just going off assumptions here."

Jack shifted in his seat, pulling his arm down from the back of the pew. He rested his elbows against his legs and leaned forward. "When did you first start having these blackout spells, Braden? I'm no expert on these things. Please don't confuse my advice or opinion for that of a medical professional. But I do want to talk this through with you."

"I'm all in favor of that." Braden let out a breath. "I suppose my issues started with tremors. But, as I got deeper into my therapy, I started having the blackouts. I assumed it was because we were talking about some pretty dark things. My therapist said my mind was trying to shut out the bad stuff."

"Does anything seem to trigger these blackouts?"

He remembered what Dr. Larson had talked to him about, remembered how he'd pinpointed issues that Braden hadn't. "Trauma, I suppose. The first night I was here, I blacked out. I found firecrackers the next morning."

Jack's eyes narrowed. "Firecrackers? Do you think someone set them off to mess with your mind?"

"It's my best guess. I assume the person who's coming after me did it."

Jack shifted. "Why would that person try to scare you? If they had the chance, why not just kill you? Why go through all this trouble instead?"

"That's a great question. I don't know. Maybe to make me miserable?"

"I know a little about terrorists. I was a soldier before I was a chaplain before I was a pastor. And terrorists usually don't have time to waste. They get the job done. Especially if it's revenge. Am I making sense?"

"You're making a little too much sense."

Jack leaned forward with his elbows against his legs. "Is there a way you can regain these memories? Has your therapist said anything about that?"

Braden shook his head. "He hasn't. But I can ask him."

"Maybe try that. Maybe there's something you can do. Because these moments when you black out —they could be key."

Maybe Jack was right. Braden only knew he had to do something.

Because he couldn't live like this for much longer.

Chapter Twenty-Three

"WHAT BRINGS YOU HERE?" Lisa asked, sitting across from Dr. Larson at one of the booths in her otherwise empty restaurant.

Almost as if on autopilot, she'd made coffee and had gotten the doctor a piece of her apple pie. She definitely didn't need to eat all three of those by herself. And Dr. Larson seemed to be enjoying his piece.

However, the anticipation over why he was here was pushing Lisa to the edge.

"I'm looking for Braden," Dr. Larson announced.

Caution reared its head. "He's not here. Why did you think he was?"

With measured, purposeful actions, he raised a

forkful of pie. "Because he mentioned you to me, Lisa. Mentioned the two of you were growing close."

"Did he?" At least that was something. Before Braden had forgotten everything, maybe what they'd had between them was real. Maybe he really had cared about her.

Lisa wasn't sure if that comforted her or only made her sadder.

"That's why I felt the need to come here and warn you." He paused from eating his pie.

All the muscles in Lisa's body seemed to stiffen at Dr. Larson's words. "Warn me? What do you mean?"

Dr. Larson put down his coffee, moved his apple pie to the side and leaned toward her. "Lisa, Braden is a very dangerous man."

She blinked, certain she hadn't heard the man correctly. "Dangerous? Braden? I mean, yes, he has some issues. But would you really consider him dangerous?"

Dr. Larson pressed his lips together in a tight line, and something resembling compassion crossed his gaze. "I'd definitely consider him dangerous. He was a trained killer, Lisa."

She gasped. "No . . ."

Braden had told her some things, but not that. Certainly it wasn't true.

"He was. And that's why he's having some of the issues he's having right now. I must say, that information isn't for the public to know. And I probably shouldn't have even told you. But I felt strongly that you needed to know that."

What was Dr. Larson's game plan here? "You came all the way here to tell me that?"

"No, I came here to talk to Braden and bring him back before he does anything else stupid. But I felt like I needed to tell you before you found yourself wrapped up in this mess he's created. Or worse —before you found yourself hurt or dead."

"He wouldn't."

"His problems are growing more serious, Lisa. As is my concern."

She leaned back, still trying to comprehend everything. "I don't know what to say. I still can't believe Braden would do this. I just can't believe it."

Dr. Larson pushed his glasses up. "Lisa, when I was a child, my family found a stray dog. The poor thing had been abandoned on a country road. It was malnourished, had mange, but his eyes drew us in. We had no idea what the dog had been through, but we were in love."

Lisa wasn't sure where Dr. Larson was going with this, but she gave him time to finish his thought. "Okay."

"We took the dog in, and I loved Bitsy. Came home every day from school, and I couldn't wait to see her. The problem was, no matter how much I loved on Bitsy, there were parts of her my love could never conquer."

"What do you mean?" His little analogy now had Lisa fully uncomfortable as she wondered where he was going with this.

"I mean that, because of what Bitsy had been through while growing up, her brain was wired differently. I don't know what happened to her as a puppy, but that dog fiercely loved the ones in our family. But anyone else? She would take them down in a minute. One day, she bit my best friend."

"I'm sorry to hear that." Her gut twisted tighter, and the few bites of the apple pie she'd tasted now felt rotten in her stomach.

"And that was it for Bitsy."

"What are you getting at, Dr. Larson?" Lisa thought she knew, but she didn't want to acknowledge the conclusions she was drawing. They were too demeaning, not to mention too difficult to face.

"Sometimes we can do everything within our

power to change someone. We can hope and believe. We can pour out our love. But that doesn't change the fiber of who a person is. It doesn't change their past or their reactions to the present."

A feeling of dread settled in her gut. "You're saying I should stay away from Braden?"

"I'm saying that I know you believe the best for Braden. He has some really kind and intriguing sides to him. But all of that attention and belief you pour into him doesn't mean he'll ever be the whole person who's ready to be committed and to return to a normal life."

Her heart lurched. "I don't know what to say."

"I can't speak specifics about my client. I just know that he's unstable, at best. I would be very careful around him."

"Thanks for your advice."

He stood. "Thank you for the coffee and pie. It was tasty, for sure. I'm going to go pay Braden a visit now. Hopefully I can talk some sense into him."

Braden stood on the screened-in porch at Hope

House, staring out over the water, and reflecting on his conversation with Jack.

It had felt good to get everything off his chest. Jack hadn't judged or looked down on him. No, they'd prayed together, and then Jack had driven him home. Once there, he'd called Mac and told him that he'd found those copper wires in his trash can. Mac was sending someone out later.

A sound drew Braden's attention. He turned toward the noise and saw a car pulling down the lane.

To his surprise, he saw a polished red SUV.

He knew exactly who it was. Rick Larson. His therapist.

What was Dr. Larson doing here in Lantern Beach?

He didn't move, just listened as the tires crunched gravel. As the engine shut off and a door opened. A moment later, footsteps came up his wooden stairs, and Dr. Larson appeared on the other side of the screen door.

"Braden," he said, pushing his glasses up higher and offering a hesitant but compassionate smile.

Braden nodded in return. "Doctor. Come in. What brings you here?"

Dr. Larson stepped onto the porch, looking out

of place with his suit jacket and button-up shirt. "I'm worried about you."

"Why are you worried about me?" Braden knew there were a lot of possible reasons—but none that should have brought the doctor here.

"Because I can hear you slipping further away each time we talk on the phone. I don't think that taking a break from our appointments for this long is a good idea. You still need a lot of help."

"I think being here is helping me." Even as Braden said the words, he wasn't sure they were true.

"Maybe it is. But so are our sessions. So is your medication. I need to make sure you stay on track."

"I'm fine, Doctor." What he wanted was to be left alone. That was why Braden had come here. Yet nothing had gone the way he planned.

"No more blackouts?"

Braden ran a hand over his face, wishing he could deny the allegation. "I've had some blackouts."

"Maybe we should up your medication."

Braden sliced his hand through the air. "No! I don't want to medicate myself even more. Whenever I take that stuff, I feel like half a person. I can't stand it."

"You know it's important."

"I know. And I'm taking the dosages you told me to take. But I'm not interested in increasing those." Braden shook his head. "I'm sorry you came all the way out here for nothing, Doctor."

Dr. Larson said nothing for a moment. "Did you have anything to do with that man who was beaten?"

Braden's spine stiffened. So this was what it really boiled down to. Had someone called the doctor here for an intervention? Who? "How did you hear about that?"

"It's been all the buzz since I arrived on the island. Even on the ferry over people were talking about it. It's a small town here. News travels fast."

"I didn't do it."

Dr. Larson nodded toward his hands. "Then what happened?"

"I don't know." Braden was tired of answering that question. Tired of not knowing.

Dr. Larson stepped closer and lowered his voice. "Braden, I'm afraid that you're going to become violent toward yourself."

Braden blinked, uncertain if he'd heard correctly. "What do you mean?"

"I mean, I've seen things like this too many

times, and I know how it ends. I don't want you to be one of those people."

"You mean, suicide? You're afraid I'm going to kill myself?" How could he even say that?

Dr. Larson raised his hand, as if to halt the thought. "I didn't say it that way exactly."

"But that's what you're implying." Adrenaline—and anger—pumped through Braden.

"I'm only saying I've seen it before." His voice sounded placating and irritatingly calm. "All the right factors are in place, and now you come here alone?"

"Is that what this is really about? You're afraid I came here to end it all? Would that tarnish your professional reputation or something?"

"No, Braden. I just want the best for you. You know I feel a personal connection to your story."

Thomas's death had connected them all. Braden had felt like part of the family as he wandered through grief with them. It was a bond only death could bring. But maybe seeing him as a therapist was a mistake. Maybe there were too many personal connections.

"I'm not the enemy," Dr. Larson said.

"I know. I just . . . I need some time right now."

He took a step back. "Well, I'll be staying at the

inn in town. If you need me, you can find me there. Or you can call, and I can be here in a few minutes. I'm staying until Thursday. I made the long trip here—there's no need for me to turn around and go right back."

"Thanks, Doc." Guilt bit at Braden a moment. Had he overreacted? And was that overreaction a sign that Braden was on edge—on the verge of doing something destructive? He didn't know.

"You're welcome, Braden."

After Dr. Larson walked away, Braden leaned against the frame of the porch.

Was he losing his mind? Was he the only one who couldn't see it? Because he didn't beat up that man. He wasn't thinking about ending it all.

But everyone around him seemed to have a different perspective.

Dear Lord, please help me. Because maybe I am losing it.

Chapter Twenty-Four

AGAINST LISA'S BETTER JUDGMENT, she found herself at Braden's place at 10:00 p.m. that evening. Blinding darkness surrounded her—darkness like that only found on an isolated island that jutted into the Atlantic. A place void of streetlights and filled with dark, empty houses. A sleepy community filled with pirate folklore and buried secrets from the past.

Before knocking on the door, she reached into the pocket of her jeans and felt the bullet casing there.

The one Braden had given her.

It reminds me of the battlefield. Of how hard that time in my life was, but how necessary for the bigger picture—the picture outside myself. When I think about that, it gives me the strength to make the right choices, even when those choices are unpleasant or hard.

Wes and Austin's trucks were in the driveway, so Lisa knew she wouldn't be here with Braden alone. She knew she probably shouldn't be here at all. But she couldn't *not* do anything.

She wouldn't stay long—just long enough to get a better feel for the situation.

The voice in her head turned into Dr. Larson's. His words echoed in her ears.

Sometimes we can do everything within our power to change someone. We can hope and believe. We can pour out our love. But that doesn't change the fiber of who a person is. It doesn't change their past or their reactions to the present.

Lisa didn't want to believe that, though. Maybe it made her a fool. An optimist. Some might even say it made her stupid.

But she didn't view Braden as a dog who'd lived on the streets too long and who'd never be normal.

And it angered her that anyone would think of Braden that way.

She'd seen Braden's eyes—the windows to his soul, as some said. And she'd observed someone who was good and kind and compassionate.

In the end, she had to trust her gut and stop listening to everyone else's voice.

Including John Linksi's, something internal said.

That was right. Lisa had to shut out the voices of the critics also. She had to focus on the call God had placed on her life and the path she'd chosen to walk.

Life was too short to second-guess herself. To listen to naysayers. To not take risks.

Which could be why Lisa was here now.

She needed to take this risk.

She knocked at the door and, a moment later, Wes answered. His eyes widened, and he leaned against the doorframe, effectively blocking her from entering.

"Lisa. What are you doing here?"

"I want to be a part of this," she announced, stepping under his arm.

Wes gently grabbed her wrist and lowered his voice. "I don't know if it's a good idea that you're here."

"I'm only staying for a little while."

"Lisa . . ."

She raised a hand to stop his thought. "I know how it might seem. But I feel like I'm the only one here on this island who believes in Braden. I need to see for myself what's going on."

"Are you sure it's not just because you have a

crush on him?"

Lisa wanted to deny it. And to call it a crush seemed too superficial. What had happened between them was much more than that.

Or was it?

She and Braden had only known each other a few days. It was too short of a time period to be more than a crush.

Yet she knew her feelings went deeper than that.

"I'm sure," she said.

Just then, Braden stepped from the hallway into the great room.

His eyes lit when he saw her. "Lisa."

She nodded, resisting the urge to step toward him. "Braden."

"What brings you here?"

She held up the bag in her hands. Food was always a great excuse to stop by. "I have more of that leftover pie. I'm trying to stop myself from eating too much of it."

"Leftover pie?"

Her heart sank. Of course he didn't remember it. What had she been thinking?

"I was doing some experiments, and I thought you might all like to try some of them."

"I'm always game." Austin took the bag from

her. "I don't mind if I do."

"Great. I'll help serve it."

She went into the kitchen and drew in a deep breath, hoping she didn't regret any of this.

As Braden bit into his piece of apple pie, a flash of memory hit him.

A memory of the taste.

Of eating this pie.

As he closed his eyes, he saw blankets. Pillows. Candlelight.

He saw stars and darkness outside.

But it was the feeling in his gut that stood out the most.

A feeling of contentment and joy.

What . . . ?

Was this a memory? Or a dream?

He had no idea.

"What is it?" Lisa asked. She sat beside him at the kitchen table, only a bottle of water in front of her as she watched his face intently.

Wes and Austin had taken their pie and were talking quietly on the other side of the room—probably talking about him. But he didn't care.

Braden shook his head. "I don't know. I feel like I've eaten this pie before . . . and somehow there's a lot of joy surrounding the memory."

A small smile played on Lisa's lips. "Is that right? Maybe you have."

He studied her, curious about her reaction. "Have I had this pie before?"

She nodded. "You have."

"Was I with you?"

She nodded again. "You were."

Lisa was one mystery he wanted to solve. Braden wanted to ask her if there had been more to their relationship. But, if there had been, wouldn't she have told him? Why would he block all those memories out? It made no sense.

He pressed his lips together, deciding not to ask any more for now. Austin and Wes were here. Even though they were caught up in their own conversation about some possible new development on the island, this just didn't feel like the time or place.

"This is really fantastic," he told Lisa instead, eating his last bite.

Her cheeks reddened. "Thanks."

As Wes and Austin joined them with empty plates, Braden cleared his throat. "Listen, I appreciate all of you being here for me. I realize you don't really know me, and I know this isn't convenient."

"It's not a problem," Wes said. "We'd hope someone would do it for us if the roles were reversed."

"I thought you should know that my therapist stopped by today." Braden had to be honest with them. What if their lives were in danger? How would he ever forgive himself? He couldn't. That was why he didn't want to hold anything back.

"Is everything okay?" Lisa asked, her eyes holding an unreadable emotion. Concern? Maybe. But there was something more.

"I guess he felt like my condition was serious enough that it warranted a special trip out here to try and convince me to leave." Braden paused and glanced at everyone here. "I felt like you all deserved the heads-up that he thinks I'm unstable. I'll understand if no one wants to stay here this evening."

"That's why Wes and I are staying here together," Austin said. "Safety in numbers."

"I just don't want to put either of you in a position that you shouldn't be in."

"We appreciate that," Wes said. "But we're in this. We want answers just as much as you."

"I appreciate that." Braden stood. "That said, let me get this cleaned up. And thank you all again."

Lisa stood also. "You mind if I use your bathroom real quick before I go?"

"Not at all. You know where it is, right?"

"Right."

———

Lisa stared at herself in the bathroom mirror a moment. Stared at her gaze, which was full of worry. Stared at the circles forming beneath her eyes.

The past few days were taking a toll on her. But it was mostly the fact that Braden had forgotten just how special the bond they'd shared had been.

And then there was Dr. Larson's visit.

His warning.

All the uncertainties.

Yes, Lisa had just said life was too short to second-guess herself. But putting that into practice as an active belief was much harder than simply believing it.

She splashed some water on her face, grabbed a clean towel from the cabinet, and dried her face. As she did, the pill bottles on the counter caught her eye.

She knew she shouldn't do it. But she still found herself picking one up.

The name of a medication she'd never seen—and that she definitely couldn't pronounce—stared back.

What was this? And why was Braden taking so many? There must be eight different kinds of prescriptions here.

She was no expert in these things. If at all possible, she tried not to take medication. She believed that often the side effects were worse than the actual diagnosis.

But she understood that sometimes a person had no other choice. That medicines could save lives.

She wasn't sure why, but she used her phone to take photos of the different pill bottle labels. She was going to do her own homework this evening.

Lisa knew she was crossing major boundaries by doing this. But she had to have some answers, and she hoped Braden would forgive her for digging into his business.

She slipped her phone back into her pocket. But guilt had already begun to eat away at her.

As she joined everyone else in the living room, she attempted to smile like nothing was wrong. "Well, I'll be going. I hope things go well here tonight."

"Do you mind if I walk you out?" Braden asked.

"No, that would be fine." Actually, it delighted her.

They stepped outside, into the brisk darkness. Neither said anything as they walked down the stairs to the drive below. Down here, it was even darker. The stars and moonlight were concealed, making it either more romantic, more dangerous, or both.

Braden paused in front of her car, his eyes seeming to swim with questions. "Why do I feel like there's more between us?"

Lisa's breath caught. Even if Braden's mind didn't remember, his heart did, didn't it?

Lisa said nothing. The words caught in her throat and wouldn't exit.

Braden stepped nearer, the energy coming from him seeming to draw them closer. "There was, wasn't there?"

Lisa nodded, even though the action took much more effort than it should have. "Yes, there was."

"But those memories are blocked."

"Yes, they are."

He reached for her, his body bent in agony as he rasped, "I want to remember."

"I want you to remember too." Before she could question herself, she reached up and rested her hands on his face, relishing the feel of his scruffy beard beneath her fingers.

Braden seemed to instinctively put his hands on her waist and pull her even closer.

There was really nothing she could say. Instead, she stood on her tiptoes and reached up for him. Lisa pressed her lips against his. Quickly—but long enough. And then she pulled away and stepped toward her car.

Her heart couldn't handle going through this again. Of having him not remember. Of trying to remind him how great they'd been.

"Goodnight, Braden." She opened her car door, about to step inside.

Braden stood there, a stupefied look on his face. He said nothing, only watched her.

But there was nothing left to be said.

Lisa climbed into her car and drove home, her thoughts battering her from the inside out.

Chapter Twenty-Five

FIRST THING IN THE MORNING, Lisa called Wes. She wore the remnants of her sleepless night in the circles beneath her eyes and her limp hair. But she didn't care.

She was showered and dressed and perched on her couch, anxious to jump into the day. "How did things go last night?"

"It was fine," Wes said, hints of weariness in his own voice. "Braden was in his bedroom all night. We didn't hear anything from him. It was . . . uneventful."

Lisa's heart pounded in her ears. "That's good news—right?"

"I guess so. We know he didn't sneak out and

wreak mayhem all over the island or commit any other crimes, for that matter."

She released the air from her lungs. She'd take whatever information she could get. "Thanks for doing that, Wes. I appreciate it."

"It's not a problem. Austin and I are both going to run in a minute. Braden said he's going to stay in today and try to rest."

As soon as Lisa hung up with Wes, she called Doc Clemson. He was the island's doctor—and, by default, the island's medical examiner. But he was also a regular customer at the Crazy Chefette, and he'd grown to be a friend.

"What's going on, Lisa? You have a new recipe you want to tell me about? I can help you name it. Heart Attack on a Plate. Acid Reflux but It's Worth It. Shave Years Off Your Life but Die Happy."

She chuckled—but barely. "Not quite. I actually have a question about some medication that I was hoping you could answer."

"I can't speak specifically about any patients of mine, you know."

"Don't worry—I'm not asking you to. These are just generic questions, if you wouldn't mind."

"You give me a piece of that apple pie Mac told me about, and you got it."

Lisa smiled. "It's a deal. This is what I'm wondering about."

She read the names of the medications Braden was taking. She'd done her own research last night, but it had been hard to find definitive answers—especially about mixing medications. She knew she had to talk to someone in-the-know if she really wanted the truth.

Mixing ingredients for crazy food combinations? That was fun.

Mixing drugs? That was a recipe for disaster.

"Hmm . . . that's an interesting mix you have going on there. I'm not sure what this is pertaining to, but I can say that those are drugs commonly used for anxiety, sleep, and pain."

"So these are drugs you're familiar with?"

"Yes, they're prescribed quite often. But please tell me someone you know isn't taking all of them at once?"

"What do you mean?"

"I mean, some of those drugs should never be mixed or combined with others. Everyone's body chemistry is different . . . making these projections unpredictable, at best. Lethal, at worst."

"Could they make a person go crazy?"

"I would say so. I'll do some more research and

get back with you. I like to double-check my facts first."

"Thanks, Doc." As Lisa hung up, the bad feeling in her gut grew.

Was that what all of this boiled down to? Were Braden's drugs the problem? Were they hindering him instead of helping his symptoms?

And, if that was case, how had this happened?

Had his general care physician not compared notes with his therapist? Had this been a careless mistake? Lisa had heard before about the care some veterans received at the military hospitals—it was subpar, at best. Was that what happened here?

She didn't know.

But a new fire lit in her blood.

Lisa had to find out. She'd been so concerned about the drugs themselves that she hadn't paid attention to the prescribing physician. He should be listed on the label.

Before she could do anything else, there was a knock at her door.

It was Mac, and he didn't look happy.

"There's something I need to tell you," he started. "And it's about Braden."

Braden stood on the porch, his head feeling clearer than it had in months.

He hadn't taken his medications last night. Yes, Dr. Larson had emphasized that he needed to. He'd told Braden about the dire repercussions that might be experienced if Braden missed just one dose.

But right now, Braden would take the anxiety. The pain. The sleeplessness. He'd take those ailments if it meant things would make sense. He figured the best time to test his theory was while Austin and Wes were there.

As the tremors started in his hands, something tried to return to his memory.

Mind over matter. Dissecting the truth from the lies. Listening to the voice of truth and allowing it to drown out everything else.

It was the recipe for change.

Who had told him that?

Flashes of memories seemed to want to return to him. He couldn't explain it. But images—images that almost seemed like dreams—kept flashing in his mind.

Memories of kissing someone.

Eating apple pie.

Feeling overflowing with happiness.

And Lisa.

Whenever he thought of any of those things, Lisa's image was somehow connected.

Braden raked a hand through his hair.

She'd kissed him last night, and her touch had seemed to spark something inside his brain. He hadn't wanted to let her go—and he had no idea why. He only had vague inclinations that they were more than mere friends.

And not remembering those details frustrated him the most.

He stared out over the dunes and drew in a deep breath. Maybe he'd take a quick walk to the ocean. It was cold outside today. Bitterly cold. But he didn't care. He needed to try and clear his head.

But first he went inside to grab his phone. He'd left it on his bedside table, where he charged the cell every night. But the device was gone.

What? Had he misplaced it? He found that hard to believe.

Braden looked a few more places but couldn't find the phone. When had he made a call last?

He couldn't remember.

He raked a hand through his hair again. Apparently, he needed that walk by the ocean now more than ever.

Listening to the waves, feeling the salty air,

enjoying the sand beneath his feet—that could be the best therapy sometimes. As his memory issues continued to plague him, that seemed like the best medicine.

Braden decided to look for his phone later. For now, he trudged down the stairs and began crossing the dune at a path that cut through the grass.

As he crested the incline, something buried in the grass caught his eye.

What was that?

Out of curiosity, he slipped between the sea oats to retrieve the objects. He leaned down and picked them up. A hammer and sandpaper.

Had the people who'd done construction on Ty's house left this here?

He turned the sandpaper over.

A dark reddish-brown stain was there.

His breath caught.

Was that blood?

Braden looked at the hammer as well. Remains of some kind of liquid had dried on the edges.

Blood.

He was sure of it.

He glanced at his hands—his bruised and sore hands.

His throat went dry. Had these objects been used by someone to make his hands look like this?

It sounded crazy.

Yet it didn't sound crazy at all.

What was going on here?

Because maybe this wasn't about terrorists bent on killing him.

No, maybe this was more about someone bent on ruining Braden's life.

But who?

Who else had he made angry enough to do this?

He had a feeling that the memory was just out of his grasp.

Chapter Twenty-Six

"YOU CAN'T BE SERIOUS," Lisa said, staring at Mac. They hadn't moved beyond the back entrance to her restaurant, and now she felt floored, like her feet had grown roots.

Mac nodded grimly. "I wish I weren't."

She leaned back against the wall, feeling light-headed. "I don't know what to say."

"All I know is that a gun was found in a ditch near where John Linski was attacked. The bullet found after someone shot out your window matches the ballistics of this gun."

"And the gun is registered to Braden Dillinger," Lisa finished, hating the grinding feeling in her gut.

Mac offered a tight-lipped smile. "Unfortu-nately, yes."

She reached into her pocket and pulled out that bullet casing Braden had given her. She'd thought it had been a beautiful symbol of hope. But had Braden actually been taunting her this whole time?

"Please tell me this doesn't match also." Her voice cracked as she said the words.

Mac took it from her, studied it, and then glanced up, a new gleam in his gaze. "Where did you get this?"

She didn't want to answer but she did anyway. "Braden gave it to me."

His frown grew larger. "It matches, Lisa. And there's one other thing."

"What's that?"

"We found a phone nearby and managed to pull up the messages. Lisa, it sounds like Braden may have been conspiring with someone to scare you. There were some unusual texts and even a picture of you."

"A picture of me?" The blood drained from her face.

"It was taken from the outside of the restaurant. At night."

"Yeah, I remember a stranger doing that. Are you saying it was Braden this whole time?"

"I'm saying that's what it looks like."

Lisa's face went into her hands. "Why did Braden goad me this whole time? Did he give this to me to rub it in that I was naïve?"

"I don't know. But I'm getting a warrant right now for his arrest."

"You're arresting him? For this? Or for John?"

"John still isn't awake. But our case is growing against Braden, as far as him committing that crime as well."

"I just didn't think this was possible. I've been defending him." Her heart felt like it was deflating inside her.

"I know you have, Lisa. And I'm sorry. I know this isn't what you want to hear. But I would stay away from him. It appears he's not the man you think he is."

Someone rapped on the door and nearly made Lisa jump out of her skin. She turned and saw Doc Clemson's face through the glass atop the back door. Quickly, she let him inside.

"Is everything okay?" she rushed.

"I'm not sure." He pulled his gloves off but gone was his normal jovial personality. "I researched those medications, and I wanted to tell you face-to-face what I found out."

She braced herself for whatever he was going to

say. The day had already been a doozy, and she had a feeling it wouldn't get much better from here. "Okay . . ."

"Lisa, the effects of mixing those prescriptions would cause someone to have a psychotic reaction."

"What?"

Doc Clemson nodded. "If your friend—or whoever is taking these medications—is taking all of them at the same time, the results could be catastrophic."

Her heart pounded in her ears as she absorbed his words. "Wouldn't the doctors have known that?"

"I'd hope so. Who's his or her doctor?"

"I don't know about his general physician. But I think his therapist prescribed some, if not most, of them. I was just going to check the labels again to see. I have photos on my phone."

"You're talking about Braden, aren't you?" Mac asked.

Lisa shrugged, guilt pressing on her. "He's not aware that I saw his medications. But his therapist is in town. Just showed up yesterday. Dr. Larson."

"Dr. Larson?" Clemson said. "He has thick glasses and thinning gray hair, right?"

"That's right. How do you know him?"

"I met him on the ferry. His wallet fell out, and,

when I picked it up for him, I saw his name on his driver's license."

"You were on the ferry yesterday?"

"No, that was three days ago . . ."

Lisa sucked in a breath, and her gaze swerved toward Mac. "We need to go to Braden's. Now."

"I'm going to call the rental agencies and see if we can find out where this Dr. Larson guy is staying," Mac said. "I'd suggest you stay away from Braden for now—until we know what's going on."

Doc's pager went off, and he glanced down at it. "And I just got called back to the clinic. No rest for the weary."

"You stay here, Lisa, okay?" Mac said, a fatherly tone to his voice. "Until we know something, you need to stay put with your doors locked. The situation could turn ugly."

She nodded, understanding the gravity of this ordeal all too well. "Okay . . . I will. But Braden . . ."

He was in danger. Did he even realize any of this? Everything that had happened . . . he'd been set up, hadn't he?

"The safest place he can be is at the police station. Trust me on this one."

Her throat tightened, but she tried to hold her anxiety back. "Okay. Thanks, you guys."

As they left, Lisa locked the door behind them. Her heart pounded out of control.

The whole picture hadn't come together in her mind, but what she did see, she didn't like. Was Dr. Larson somehow responsible for what was going on with Braden? If so, why? What motive could he possibly have?

She couldn't sit still. She had too much energy. Too much to think about. Instead, she paced into the dining area.

As soon as Lisa stepped past the kitchen door, she heard a step behind her and then a click.

Slowly, breathlessly, she pivoted.

Dr. Larson stood there, a gun in his hand.

Chapter Twenty-Seven

"GOOD MORNING," someone called in the distance.

Braden looked over and saw Pastor Jack standing on the beach. He clenched the items in his hands before shoving the sandpaper into his pocket and the hammer through his belt.

He tried to say something to Jack. But the flashes were coming faster, more quickly.

His hands went to his temples, and he squeezed his eyes shut.

What kind of memories were there? They were so close to coming into focus.

"Braden?" Jack asked, pausing at the base of the sand dune and looking concerned. "I was just taking a walk and . . ."

Braden didn't hear the rest of what he said. No, suddenly, Braden was back in the small apartment in France.

France?

Yes, he was working a job for the military. Black ops.

If he was discovered, the government would deny they'd authorized the mission.

This was a meeting place for The Revolt. They'd gone outside American soil to plan their missions.

He opened a drawer and saw a black notebook inside. He opened it.

Names were listed there.

Names of Revolt members.

He scanned them, holding the book closer so he could see in the darkness of the room.

His gaze stopped at one name.

Was that . . .?

No, it couldn't be.

But it was.

He knew someone on this list. He knew a member of The Revolt.

But . . . how could this person betray his country like this?

He shoved the book into his pocket as he heard a noise outside the apartment.

He had to get out of here.

Moving quickly, he headed toward the window. He'd leave down the fire escape.

But just as he shoved the window open, an explosion sounded.

And it was the last thing Braden had remembered until he woke up in a military hospital.

And the book had been gone.

"Braden?" Jack repeated.

Braden jerked his gaze toward the pastor. "I need your help."

"Sure thing. What's going on?"

"Can you give me a ride somewhere? Right now?"

"Of course. Let's go."

Lisa sucked in a breath, wondering if Dr. Larson had been there long enough to hear all of her conversation with Mac and Doc Clemson. Her guess was that he had.

"How did you get inside?" Her voice trembled.

Malice gleamed in his eyes. "It's really not that hard to pick a lock."

"Why would you do this?" She stepped back, looking around for a weapon. There was nothing. Nothing. All her knives were located on the other side of the breakfast bar, well out of reach.

"You shouldn't worry your pretty little head over that."

"Considering you have a gun pointed at me, I think I will. I gave you pie, and this is your response?"

He chuckled. "Good one. But pie doesn't fix everything."

"My grandma always said it did."

"She sounds charming."

Her thoughts shifted from trying to change his mind to trying to figure out what he was thinking. "What are you going to do with me?"

He shrugged. "You know too much. At first, I just wanted to frighten you. But now it's apparent that I have to do more."

"You don't have to do anything."

"It's more complicated than that."

A sound cut through the tension. It almost sound like a hand. Hitting glass.

Lisa jerked her head toward the front of the restaurant.

Braden.

Braden stood there.

He pressed himself into the door and pounded. His eyes looked full of rage.

"Let me in!" he shouted.

Dr. Larson laughed, not the least bit flustered by Braden's presence. "I kind of figured this would happen."

Braden. Braden was here.

But would he be able to help in time?

"Why are you doing this?" Lisa asked, taking a step back.

Could she run? No, the door was too far away. And the doctor had a gun.

"It's a long story," Dr. Larson said. "I'd love to fill you in, but I might have to bill you. I'm pretty expensive per hour."

The coldness by which he said the words sent another shiver up her spine. He was determined to see this through, and he didn't seem to have any emotions to appeal to. Lisa didn't know much about criminals, but he seemed like the most dangerous kind.

"You were behind all of this. You set Braden up. You wanted him to take the blame for everything."

The corner of his lip twitched, like he wanted to smile. "There's a certain art to being subtle. I figured this would be the ultimate justice. Braden could take the fall for everything—from John to those stupid copper wires. I messed with his mind. Did everything I could to push him over the edge. But when he met you, all of that seemed to fall by the wayside."

Her gaze swerved back toward Braden.

He was gone. He had disappeared from the door.

Lisa's heart pounded even harder. Where had he gone? Had he given up?

Then she heard something slam in the rear of the building.

The back door, she realized. Braden was coming in through the back door.

A temporary sag of relief caught her by surprise.

The doctor lunged at her. Before she realized what was happening, Dr. Larson grabbed her arm. She sucked in a quick breath as he shoved the gun to her head.

This man could kill her. Easily. With just a jerk of his finger.

"Let her go." Braden's voice sounded steely as he stepped from the back of the restaurant.

Satisfaction lit the doctor's voice. "Why would I do that? I already have a great story worked out. One where you kill Lisa before killing yourself. I'll be here to witness it all and testify to what happened. Of course, I'll say I tried to stop you."

Braden's jaw flexed. "Because I remembered. I remembered everything. And now we need to end this."

Chapter Twenty-Eight

BRADEN STARED DOWN THE DOCTOR, disgust boiling inside him.

"You didn't remember anything." Dr. Larson practically spit out the words, an air of self-righteousness about him.

"Oh, but I did. I remembered all of it."

"It's not possible!"

Being off his medication had pushed away some of the clouds from Braden's mind. Then he'd realized that only one person made sense as the culprit. Dr. Larson.

As Jack drove him here, Braden had used his phone to call his old commanding officer. As they'd spoken, Braden had realized that Thomas's death had affected the doctor entirely more than Braden had assumed.

Facts—and memories—began clicking in place. And, with each new fact, came a new memory. It was like doors began opening in his mind.

And he was disgusted at what he saw. At the memories the doctor had repressed.

And the reason behind everything.

"You've been drugging me and using your therapy to make me forget key moments in my life —like Lisa. But you were afraid I would remember too much one day. That's why you had to make it seem like I'm losing my mind."

"Now why would I do that?"

The smug tone in Dr. Larson's voice made Braden's skin crawl.

"Because I remembered your name was on a list I saw from The Revolt," Braden said. "You're one of them."

Lisa audibly gasped.

"Don't be ridiculous," Dr. Larson muttered. "You're out of your mind."

Braden's back stiffened at his words. He'd believed that lie for too long. "But I'm not. After Thomas was killed during the training exercise, you started to hate the country that had taken your son from you. I came to you for treatment, and you were afraid I knew. You recovered that memory, and you knew you had to do something. So you've basically been brainwashing me, as well as keeping an eye on me."

Something shifted in the doctor's eyes. "None of this was supposed to happen like this."

"No, it wasn't. You just wanted me put away. You wanted me to be charged with stalking Lisa. You wanted me to look responsible for John Linksi —you took a hammer and sandpaper to my hands."

"I must have dropped them on my way out." Dr. Larson's face darkened. "It was a sloppy mistake."

"You wanted me out of your hair. But you couldn't bring yourself to kill me." Braden glanced at Lisa. Saw the fear on her face.

His heart squeezed. He had to get her away from Dr. Larson.

But the doctor had a gun, and Braden didn't. Braden would need to choose each action very carefully.

Dr. Larson's nostrils flared. "You were Thomas's friend. You can understand where it might be difficult."

"Of course it would be difficult. But that wasn't going to stop you, if it boiled down to it."

"Do you know what will happen if authorities learn my name is on the roll for The Revolt? Everything will be ruined. My wife will never look at me in the same way again."

"You should have thought about that before you joined them."

Dr. Larson jerked Lisa closer to him, his face turning red. "Let's just make this easier and get it over with."

Lisa let out a cry as the doctor squeezed her arm.

"Don't hurt her," Braden growled. Why did the doctor have to pull her into this? She was innocent. Then again, people like Dr. Larson didn't care. They only cared about their own agendas.

"I'm sorry it has to be this way. I really am." Dr. Larson flexed the muscles in his hand, as if preparing himself to pull the trigger and end Lisa's life.

Braden raised his hand, trying to get the doctor to calm down before Lisa became a casualty here. He couldn't handle the thought of it. No, he and Lisa had so much of life ahead of them, waiting to explore. "Don't do this, Doc."

"I have to. You ruined our plan."

Braden's stomach twisted again. This whole time Braden had thought he was out of his mind. Really, it was Dr. Larson who had issues. "Your plan with The Revolt to kill thousands of people?"

Anger flashed in the doctor's eyes. "There are good people involved. We just have to get people to see our vision."

"How did you get involved? Why?" That was the one thing Braden truly didn't understand. Braden wanted answers—but he also wanted to keep the doctor talking to buy time.

"They found me after Thomas died. It started simple. A man who used the treadmill next to me at the gym. He was nice. And he was a recruiter. I told him about Thomas, and he reminded me about how angry I should be. Look what the government had done to my son! Eventually, they convinced me to become part of them."

"They just wanted to get to me, didn't they?" The thought of it made Braden sick to his stomach. How could so many people be so messed up?

Dr. Larson's face reddened. "You were my primary mission, yes. They discovered you were the one behind the thwarting of their plan. They wanted revenge. They saw me as the best way to exact that revenge. I agreed."

Lisa let out a little gasp. The doctor must be squeezing her arm tighter. Pressing the gun harder.

Braden wanted nothing more than to secure her in the safety of his arms. But he couldn't do that. Not yet.

"Thomas's death was a terrible accident, Dr. Larson. All of his colleagues mourned for him." *Calm him down, Braden. Calm him down. Buy time.*

"They didn't mourn enough!" The doctor's voice rose. "They didn't understand the loss I felt. The loss my wife felt. Someone needed to pay."

"There are better ways."

"I'm tired of talking." Dr. Larson repositioned his gun against Lisa's temple. "I'm sorry, Braden. But we just need to get this over with."

He was going to shoot Lisa, Braden realized. His heart clutched with grief. With fear. With agony.

"No!" Braden yelled.

But it was too late.

A gunshot filled the air.

Lisa waited to feel the pain and agony of being shot.

But there was nothing.

Maybe she'd gone into shock.

She had no idea.

But the next instant, Braden held her in his arms.

Dr. Larson slipped away.

And Mac came into view.

Mac?

"Are you okay?" Braden asked, studying her. His voice sounded tense and breathless, and his gaze was filled with worry.

Lisa didn't know. Was she okay? She tried to take a mental inventory. She glanced down the length of her. She didn't see any wounds. But . . . that gunshot. Was she in shock? Could she not feel anything because of it?

"I . . . I think I'm okay."

"Jack came and found me." Mac grabbed the gun from the floor. "I sneaked in through the back door and into the kitchen. I heard everything."

Lisa turned around and saw Dr. Larson on the floor, a pool of blood around his shoulder. He moaned.

Braden pulled her back, holding her in his arms, as he glanced back at his doctor.

"I'm so sorry you got dragged into this, Lisa."

She looked up at him, her heart filling with love. "I'm sorry you were pulled into it. How did you remember?"

"I had a flash of memory about a conversation regarding believing the truth and figuring out the lies in our lives. I . . . well, I didn't take my medication last night. I just wanted to see how I would feel if I didn't. I figured since your friends were there, it would be a good time to try that. I woke up with so much clarity."

"The mix you were taking . . . it was toxic."

"Yeah, I know that now. Earlier, I found evidence that someone made my hands look beat-up, and I knew there was more going on. I began having flashbacks, and I remembered seeing Dr. Larson's name on a list written by The Revolt. I was afraid he might come after you to get to me."

"I'm glad you remembered when you did. Good timing."

"God timing, I'd say."

She licked her lips, hesitant to ask her next question. But she had to know, even if the answer wasn't what she wanted. "Does that mean you remember . . ."

Braden smiled and reached for her. "Yeah, I remember you. And me. Together."

Tears pushed to her eyes. "I can't tell you how happy that makes me."

"The doctor tried to make me forget." He pulled her into his arms. "I'm so glad you're okay."

"I'm glad you're okay too."

"I'm going to be okay," he said. "For the first time in forever, I know I'm going to be okay."

Epilogue

LISA STOOD BACK from the busyness around her and smiled.

Thanksgiving dinner was going in full force here at the Crazy Chefette, and the sweet warmth of the moment wrapped around her, rivaling the comforting scent of apples, cinnamon, and bacon-wrapped turkey.

Though Lisa had fixed some of her signature crazy recipes for this event, she'd also fixed plenty of traditional ones. After all, what was Thanksgiving but a celebration of traditions? Traditions not just of food, but of giving thanks and being with loved ones.

Though she'd originally planned the feast for just her and her friends, it had turned into something more. She'd invited all of her Meals on Wheels participants—the ones who were able to get out on occasion—as well as anyone else on the island who didn't have family in town.

Her restaurant was packed.

She was thrilled to see her regular gang here, including Ty and Cassidy. Mac, Doc Clemson, Pastor Jack, and even Jimmy James, the town's lovable bad boy, were also here. Carter Denver, the island's favorite musician, played some soft guitar music in the corner—songs about finding love and being thankful to God. Skye's niece, Serena, was finally back in town, and she'd driven her ice cream truck here. If people guessed the amount of candy corn in a jar she brought, she was going to give them free ice cream for a year.

This was Lisa's vision for the restaurant. It was never just about food. It was about using food to bring people together. To practice the art of community. To be a place where people could share their lives with one another.

As she let out a contented sigh, someone's arms slipped around her from behind.

Lisa smiled as warmth filled her. She knew exactly who it was.

"Hello, Braden," she murmured.

He leaned down close—close enough that his cheek brushed hers. His familiar scent, his overpowering and protective stature, his warm voice . . . all those things made a burst of joy explode inside her.

"This looks like a rousing success," he murmured in her ear.

"I'd say so."

Braden was doing so much better now that a reputable therapist had taken control of his medications. He was well on track for weaning himself off many of his prescriptions. With the change in his Rx, so many of his issues had gone away.

For the time being, he was staying in one of the spare bedrooms at Jack's place. He was helping Ty with the remodel during the week and helping Lisa at the restaurant on weekends.

Maybe when he was cleared by his new therapist, he would apply for a position with either the Lantern Beach Police Department or the Coast Guard. He wasn't sure yet. But Lisa knew he'd figure it out.

As the door opened, Lisa sucked in a breath.

John Linksi stepped inside. He walked with a cane while his leg recovered, and his face still didn't look quite normal—it was swollen and pale with several cuts that were still healing.

But he was here. And he was walking.

And . . . Lisa had invited him.

John's gaze went to her, and Lisa braced herself. She hadn't talked to the man much since the incident that put him in the hospital, and she wasn't sure how he would act being here. Like a crazy drunk? Like a hard-to-please critic?

For a split moment, she second-guessed herself. Maybe inviting him wasn't a good idea.

As if Braden could read her mind, he squeezed her arm. "You've got this."

And she did. With Braden by her side, she felt like she could handle almost anything that was thrown at her.

John paused in front of her and said nothing for a minute. Finally, he cleared his throat and simply stated, "Thank you."

Lisa licked her lips. "You're welcome. How are you feeling?"

"My recovery is right on progress."

"I'm glad the person who did this to you is going away for life," Braden said.

Yes, that was right. Dr. Rick Larson wouldn't be experiencing freedom for a long time. Not only after what he did to Braden and John, but because of his affiliation with The Revolt.

John shifted. "Look, I need to say I'm sorry, Lisa. I know I was hard on you."

"I understand that not everyone is going to be on board with my philosophy of cooking and eating."

He shook his head. "It's not even that. Honestly, you're doing what I've always wanted to do. You're not afraid to take risks. What did I always do? I hid behind my criticisms. And I'm bitter toward people who are living my dream."

Lisa's throat tightened at his honesty. It was the last thing she'd expected. "It's never too late."

He shrugged. "You're right. It's not. Right now, I have to get myself together. After my wife left five years ago, I turned to drinking. Too much drinking, as you might have guessed. I'm ready to turn myself around. I can't let one person control me this much."

"I agree."

He released his breath. "Anyway, thanks for having me. It looks like it's time to eat."

Lisa nodded. "We've already prayed over the food and everything, so help yourself."

As he walked away, Braden nudged her around to face him. Everyone around them seemed to disappear until it was just her and Braden.

"You're one amazing woman, you know that?" Braden murmured.

"Feel free to tell me over and over again. I like affirmation." Lisa grinned. "I wish I were joking, but I'm not. Really—feel free to tell me."

He chuckled. "You're one amazing woman."

"You're pretty amazing yourself."

He leaned toward her and planted a kiss on her lips.

Her entire body melted with warmth—like a gooey chocolate sundae with espresso grounds on top.

Lisa knew it seemed too soon to be in love with this man. But she also knew that she loved him. Beyond a doubt.

Somehow, they were both better when they were together.

And her earlier theory was right. Sometimes in life, if you settled for what was good enough, then you would never know what could be better.

God had brought her someone who was so much better than she could have ever dreamed. And she would be thankful for that for the rest of her life.

Also by Christy Barritt:

Hidden Currents

You can take the detective out of the investigation, but you can't take the investigator out of the detective. A notorious gang puts a bounty on Detective Cady Matthews's head after she takes down their leader, leaving her no choice but to hide until she can testify at trial. But her temporary home across the country on a remote North Carolina island isn't as peaceful as she initially thinks. Living under the new identity of Cassidy Livingston, she struggles to keep her investigative skills tucked away, especially after a body washes ashore. When local police bungle the murder investigation, she can't resist stepping in. But Cassidy is supposed to be keeping a low profile. One wrong move could lead to both her discovery and her demise. Can she bring justice to the island . . . or will the hidden currents surrounding her pull her under for good?

Flood Watch

The tide is high, and so is the danger on Lantern Beach. Still in hiding after infiltrating a dangerous gang, Cassidy Livingston just has to make it a few more months before she can testify at trial and resume her old life. But trouble keeps finding her, and Cassidy is pulled into a local investigation after a man mysteriously disappears from the island she now calls home. A recurring nightmare from her time undercover only muddies things, as does a visit from the parents of her handsome ex-Navy SEAL neighbor. When a friend's life is threatened, Cassidy must make choices that put her on the verge of blowing her cover. With a flood watch on her emotions and her life in a tangle, will Cassidy find the truth? Or will her past finally drown her?

Storm Surge

A storm is brewing hundreds of miles away, but its effects are devastating even from afar. Laid-back, loose, and light: that's Cassidy Livingston's new motto. But when a makeshift boat with a bloody cloth inside washes ashore near her oceanfront home, her detective instincts shift into gear . . . again. Seeking clues isn't the only thing on her mind—romance is heating up with next-door neighbor and former Navy SEAL Ty Chambers as well. Her heart wants the love and stability she's longed for her entire life. But her hidden identity only leads to a tidal wave of turbulence. As more answers emerge about the boat, the danger around her rises, creating a treacherous swell that threatens to reveal her past. Can Cassidy mind her own business, or will the storm surge of violence and corruption that has washed ashore on Lantern Beach leave her life in wreckage?

Dangerous Waters

Danger lurks on the horizon, leaving only two choices: find shelter or flee. Cassidy Livingston's new identity has begun to feel as comfortable as her favorite sweater. She's been tucked away on Lantern Beach for weeks, waiting to testify against a deadly gang, and is settling in to a new life she wants to last forever. When she thinks she spots someone malevolent from her past, panic swells inside her. If an enemy has found her, Cassidy won't be the only one who's a target. Everyone she's come to love will also be at risk. Dangerous waters threaten to pull her into an overpowering chasm she may never escape. Can Cassidy survive what lies ahead? Or has the tide fatally turned against her?

Perilous Riptide

Just when the current seems safer, an unseen danger emerges and threatens to destroy everything. When Cassidy Livingston finds a journal hidden deep in the recesses of her ice cream truck, her curiosity kicks into high gear. Islanders suspect that Elsa, the journal's owner, didn't die accidentally. Her final entry indicates their suspicions might be correct and that what Elsa observed on her final night may have led to her demise. Against the advice of Ty Chambers, her former Navy SEAL boyfriend, Cassidy taps into her detective skills and hunts for answers. But her search only leads to a skeletal body and trouble for both of them. As helplessness threatens to drown her, Cassidy is desperate to turn back time. Can Cassidy find what she needs to navigate the perilous situation? Or will the riptide surrounding her threaten everyone and everything Cassidy loves?

Deadly Undertow

The current's fatal pull is powerful, but so is one

detective's will to live. When someone from Cassidy Livingston's past shows up on Lantern Beach and warns her of impending peril, opposing currents collide, threatening to drag her under. Running would be easy. But leaving would break her heart. Cassidy must decipher between the truth and lies, between reality and deception. Even more importantly, she must decide whom to trust and whom to fear. Her life depends on it. As danger rises and answers surface, everything Cassidy thought she knew is tested. In order to survive, Cassidy must take drastic measures and end the battle against the ruthless gang DH-7 once and for all. But if her final mission fails, the consequences will be as deadly as the raging undertow.

You might also enjoy ...

THE SQUEAKY CLEAN MYSTERY SERIES

On her way to completing a degree in forensic science, Gabby St. Claire drops out of school and starts her own crime-scene cleaning business. When a routine cleaning job uncovers a murder weapon the police overlooked, she realizes that the wrong person is in jail. She also realizes that crime scene cleaning might be the perfect career for utilizing her investigative skills.

#1 Hazardous Duty
#2 Suspicious Minds
#2.5 It Came Upon a Midnight Crime (novella)
#3 Organized Grime
#4 Dirty Deeds

When Holly Anna Paladin is given a year to live, she embraces her final days doing what she loves most—random acts of kindness. But when one of her extreme good deeds goes horribly wrong, implicating Holly in a string of murders, Holly is suddenly in a different kind of fight for her life. She knows one thing for sure: she only has a short amount of time to make a difference. And if helping the people she cares about puts her in danger, it's a risk worth taking.

The Worst Detective Ever:

I'm not really a private detective. I just play one on TV.

Joey Darling, better known to the world as Raven Remington, detective extraordinaire, is trying to separate herself from her invincible alter ego. She played the spunky character for five years on the hit TV show *Relentless*, which catapulted her to fame and into the role of Hollywood's sweetheart. When her marriage falls apart, her finances dwindle to nothing, and her father disappears, Joey finds herself on the Outer Banks of North Carolina, trying to piece together her life away from the lime-light. But as people continually mistake her for the character she played on TV, she's tasked with solving real life crimes . . . even though she's terrible at it.

About the Author

USA Today has called Christy Barritt's books "scary, funny, passionate, and quirky."

Christy writes both mystery and romantic suspense novels that are clean with underlying messages of faith. Her books have won the Daphne du Maurier Award for Excellence in Suspense and Mystery, have been twice nominated for the Romantic Times Reviewers' Choice Award, and have finaled for both a Carol Award and Foreword Magazine's Book of the Year.

She is married to her Prince Charming, a man who thinks she's hilarious—but only when she's not trying to be. Christy is a self-proclaimed klutz, an avid music lover who's known for spontaneously bursting into song, and a road trip aficionado.

When she's not working or spending time with her family, she enjoys singing, playing the guitar, and exploring small, unsuspecting towns where people have no idea how accident-prone she is.

Find Christy online at:
www.christybarritt.com
www.facebook.com/christybarritt
www.twitter.com/cbarritt

Sign up for Christy's newsletter to get information on all of her latest releases here: **www.christybarritt.com/newsletter-sign-up /**

If you enjoyed this book, please consider leaving a review.